Crystal Saga Series 4

1 – Defense = Offense

2 – Interplanetary Conflict

D. E. Weingand

Crystal Saga Series 4

1 – Defense = Offense
2 – Interplanetary Conflict

A Crystal Saga Series

ISBN: 979-8-218-46125-6

Published by D. E. Weingand, Florence, Oregon 97439.

Printed in the United States of America.

Front cover photo by D. E. Weingand. Design by Luanna K. Leisure.

Luanna K. Leisure, Little White Feather Graphic Designer, and Independent Publisher. Campbell, California.

To order additional books go to:
http://www.LuLu.com, Amazon.com or Barnesandnoble.com
Email: weingand@me.com

Defense = Offense
Crystal Saga Series 4
Book 1

Table of Contents

Map of Akura Light Side vi

Map of Akura Dark Side...vii

Setting and Geography.. viii

Cast of Characters (Arranged by kingdom)..............................xii

First Generation Super Children (and their home kingdoms)..xxiii

Second Generation Super Children (Marinea)........................xxiii

Second Generation Super Children (Mosshire) xxiv

Third Generation Super Children (Marinea)...........................xxiv

Fourth Generation Super Children (Marinea).........................xxiv

Sixth Generation Super Children (Marinea) xxv

Eighth Generation Super Children (Marinea).........................xxv

Tenth Generation Super Children (Marine) xxv

Twelfth Generation Super Children (Marine)..........................xxv

Prologue xxix

   1.   The Meeting...1

   2.   Explorer 3 7

   3.   Investigating Sabotage 13

   4.   Avatars?..17

   5.   Good Defense = Offense 23

Book 1

Table of Contents Continued

6. Learning New Ways 27

7. More Training Missions 33

8. The Training Mission 39

9. Enter the Birds 45

10. The Astral Journey 51

11. Counter Measures 57

12. The Meeting 61

13. The Defense of Akura 67

Interplanetary Conflict
Crystal Saga Series 4
Book 2

Table of Contents

Prologue iii

1. Arrival at Divos 1

2. Meanwhile, on Explorer 3 7

3. The Mission Continues................................. 13

4. Another Secret Weapon 17

5. The New Spell 23

6. Space Force 2.0.. 29

7. The Holding Cell... 35

8. The Negotiations 41

9. The Mediators Speak.................................... 45

10. Family Matters.. 49

11. The Family Celebration................................. 55

12. Change is Coming... 59

13. First Steps 63

About the Author... 69

Crystal Saga Series 1 Books by D. E. Weingand.......... 70

Crystal Saga Series 2 Books by D. E. Weingand.......... 71

Crystal Saga Series 3 Books by D. E. Weingand.......... 72

Crystal Saga Series 4 Books by D. E. Weingand.......... 73

Coming Soon... 73

AKURA

LIGHT SIDE

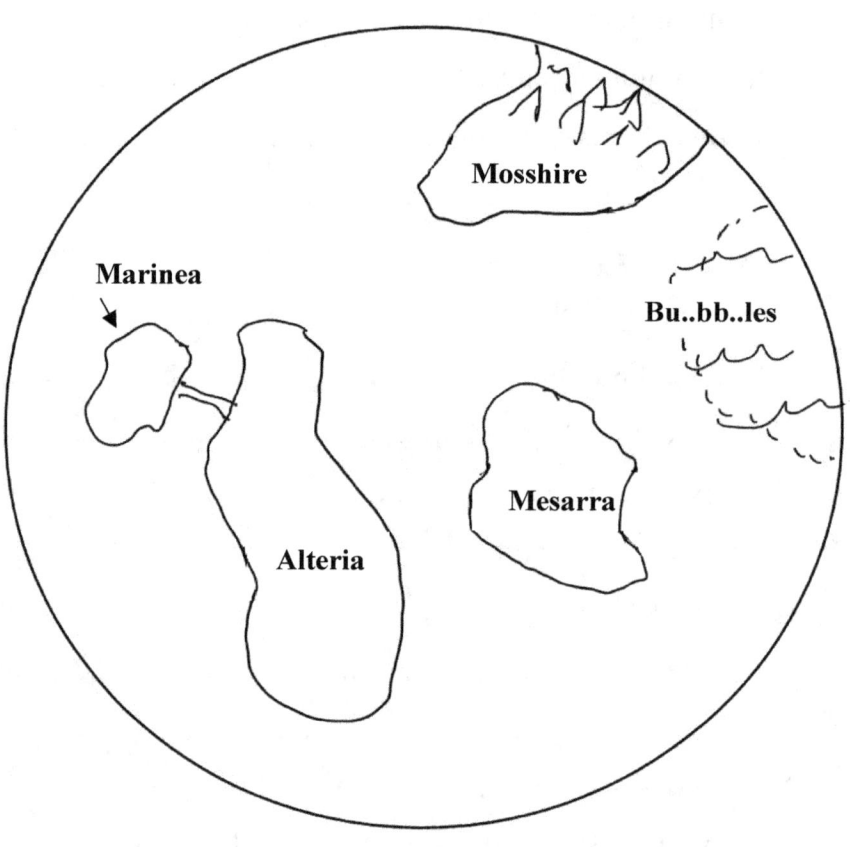

AKURA

DARK SIDE

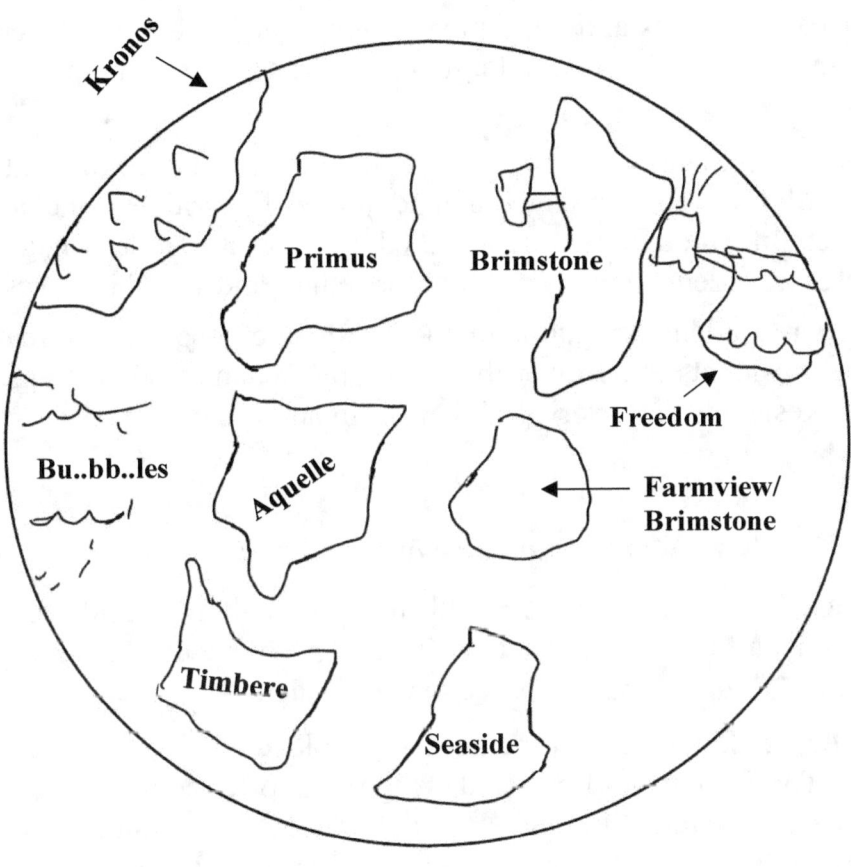

Setting and Geography

<u>Akura...A planet</u>

(On the light side of the planet)

Alteria...The land kingdom which succumbed to the Great Quakes. The remaining land portion is governed by a Council of Elders. Alterians have hazel eyes and blonde hair.

Marinea...The kingdom under the sea formed after the Great Quakes divided the land kingdom of Alteria. Marineans have silver hair and eyes and were governed by kings, now by Queen Tamara. They have retractable gills in order to live on both land and sea.

Mosshire...A land kingdom in the cold north composed of small pieces of forested, ice-covered land joined by bridges, and an impenetrable mountain range. Ruled by Sostor, an ice magic sorcerer. Residents have fair skin, blonde hair and very blue eyes.

Mesarra...A land kingdom in the south composed of a great desert. Residents are from tribes ruled by Sunan, a solar magic mage. Residents have very dark hair, skin and eyes.

*　　*　　*　　*　　*

(On the dark side of the planet)

Primus...A verdant kingdom with many greenhouses and well-designed buildings. Subject to seismic activity. Ruled by King Forty, the fortieth king in the sequence of rulers.

Aquelle...A kingdom that includes a huge lake that feeds into the ocean. There are many boats and bridges that offer connections to a series of islands. Previously ruled by King Scimitar; now governed through elections, currently by President Regis.

Timbere…A kingdom situated in a large forest with treehouses linked by aerial pathways. Ruled by Queen Flora III, a Super Sister and Twin to Queen Astrid.

*   *   *   *   *

Brimstone…A mountainous kingdom with many caves. Previously ruled by King Lucas, a wielder of shadow magic. Now ruled through election by Lucian.

Farmview…A kingdom supplying the kingdom of Brimstone, now part of Brimstone.

Freedom…An island kingdom populated by refugees from Brimstone; ruled by Cyril and his twin brother, Cyrus, both identified as Super Children/Twins.

Seaside…A kingdom on the sea. Ruled by Queen Astrid, a Super Sister and Twin of Queen Flora III.

*   *   *   *   *

Kronos…A kingdom beneath the mountain range behind Mosshire. Once ruled by King Rupert I, now deceased; presently ruled by King Rupert II, a Super Brother and Twin of Shamous from the kingdom of Marinea and owner of the magical shop **Your Every Wish.** Residents are Elves.

'Bu..bb..les'…A kingdom beneath the 'endless sea' between Kronos and Marinea. Part of both light and dark sides of Akura. Ruled by King Posidon; residents are mermaids and mermen.

*   *   *   *   *

On another astral plane…

<u>The Crystal Castle</u>

Home of the Super Beings and their Watcher/Guardians.

ix

Elsewhere in the Universe. . .

Starbright...a planet

Starlight... An alien kingdom recently ruled by a King and Queen, killed in a crash of their airship on Akura. Now succeeded by their daughter, **Trixie**, a Super Child living on the planet Akura.

Starshine... The second alien kingdom on the planet Starbright. Ruled by Queen Bella, who had been imprisoned by the leaders of a military uprising and is now freed.

*   *   *   *   *

Planet X...a planet

A planet responsible for the unsolved kidnapping of Queen Tamara and Queen-Designate Candace of Marinea. Now threatened by its star going supernova.

Bluegreen...a planet

Planet #1 in the search for a new home suitable for the residents of Planet X.

Cloudy...a planet

Planet #2 in the search for a new home suitable for the residents of Planet X.

Robotic...a planet

Planet #3 in the search for a new home suitable for the residents of Planet X.

Winner...a planet

Planet #4 in the search for a new home suitable for the residents of Planet X.

*   *   *   *   *

Divos...a planet

Location... On the other end of the galaxy; connected to Akura by a Black Hole.

Dubbell... One of two major kingdoms on the planet. Originally ruled by an unnamed Ruler. Populated by pairs of residents: one human and one avatar. Residents wear very colorful clothing.

Thalia... The second major kingdom on the planet. Ruled by Nikos. Residents wear clothing in shades of grey and beige. There is an active Resistance movement.

Communities... Population groups in early stages of political organization.

*   *   *   *   *

Planet G...a planet

Location... In another galaxy; elsewhere in the universe. Thought to be seeking more territory.

Cast of Characters (Arranged by Kingdom)

(On the light side of Akura)

Marinea

Tamara…Queen Emerita of Marinea; a First Generation Super Child and Sister/Twin to Trina. Married to Sean.

Sean…Commander Emeritus of the Marinean Security Force, Tamara's husband, and a First Generation Super Child/Twin to Jon.

Candace (Candy)… New Queen of Marinea; One of four original Super Children of Tamara and Sean. No mirror Twin. Second Generation. Wed to Cyril of Freedom. Mother of Sixth Generation Joy and Twelfth Generation fraternal Twins Fernne and Forrest. Grandmother of Savior (Savvy).

Sunny…One of four original Super Children of Queen Emerita Tamara and Commander Emeritus Sean. No Mirror Twin. Second Generation. Wed to Cyrus of Freedom.

Skye…One of four original Super Children of Queen Emerita Tamara and Commander Emeritus Sean. No Mirror Twin. Second Generation. Wed to Greta of Marinea.

Verd… One of four original Super Children of Queen Emerita Tamara and Commander Emeritus Sean. No Mirror Twin. Second Generation. Wed to Savea of Marinea. Father of Lavan and Wavan.

Leilani and **Andrea**… Second Generation Super Children/Twin daughters of Queen Emerita Tamara and Commander Emeritus Sean.

Scarlett and Pepper…The new Twelfth Generation Super Children/fraternal Twins of Queen Emerita Tamara and Commander Emeritus Sean.

* * * * *

Trina…A First Generation Super Child and Sister/Twin to Queen Emerita Tamara. Wed to Jon.

Jon...A First Generation Super Child/Twin to Commander Emeritus Sean and member of the Security Force. President of the Academy of Magic. Wed to Trina.

Tristan and **Brendan**...The Second Generation twin sons of Trina and Jon.

*   *   *   *   *

Marigold and **Steele**...Watchers/Nannies to the infant children of Tamara and Sean. New Nannies for Joy.

Pansy and **Cooper**...Watchers/Nannies to the royal children of Trina and Jon.

*   *   *   *   *

Constantine...Tutor to the first-born children of Queen Emerita Tamara and Commander Emeritus Sean and newly appointed Marinean Historian. Taken into custody by the Marinean Security Force for illegal actions at the Academy of Magic.

Crystos...New tutor to the twin girls/Super Sisters newly born to Queen Emerita Tamara and Commander Emeritus Sean. First Generation Super Child and twin to Georgio. Briefly designated Ambassador-Elect to the kingdom of Starshine. Later, also a tutor to the foster child, Trixie. Second-in-Command of the newly established Space Force.

*   *   *   *   *

Terra...Mother of Tamara and Trina, wed to Trident; also Head Watcher and non-designated Super Child.

Trident...Father of Queen Emerita Tamara and Trina; wed to Terra; formerly a Prince and King of Marinea; Ambassador to Alteria. First Generation Twin to Trillium.

Trillium...Trident's First Generation twin, and Ambassador to Mesarra. Reassigned as Ambassador to Starshine.

Solange... Mother of Trident; Grandmother of Queen Emerita Tamara and Trina; a First Generation Super Child/Twin to Savea. Wed to Sostor. Mother of Coral and Frosti, Second Generation

xiii

Super Sister/Twins/ Children of Solange and Sostor.

*   *   *   *   *

Savea…A First Generation Super Child Sister/Twin to Solange. Wed to Verd, son of Queen Emerita Tamara and Commander Emeritus Sean. Upgraded by Creation Being to a Second Generation Super Child. Mother of Lavan and Wavan.

Verd…A first-born Second Generation Super Child of Queen Emerita Tamara and Commander Emeritus Sean, wed to Savea; father of Lavan and Wavan.

Lavan and **Wavan**…Third Generation Super Twins/Brothers; children of Savea and Verd.

Daffi and **Bronze**…Watcher/Nannies to the twin sons of Savea and Verd.

*   *   *   *   *

Mia…Tamara's personal attendant.

Dr. Astarte…Royal Physician to the royal court.

Amanda…Tamara's Social Secretary.

*   *   *   *   *

Dana…Newly-appointed Second-in-Command and Leader of the Security Force.

Jon and **Borel**…Members of the Marinean Security Force's Special Task Force.

Mimi and **Clark**…New members of the Security Task Force.

Franc and **Kari**…Members of the Force selected to work with the twins to redesign the Practice Sessions.

Georgio…Experienced member of the Security Force and newly appointed tutoring assistant to Constantine in service to the royal children in the Crystal Castle. Once the children became adults, he was appointed as interim Ambassador to Mosshire and interim manager of the Academy President's office. He has completed

Graduate Studies at the Academy and finished his doctoral research. First Generation Super Child and twin to Crystos. Wed to Rose. Appointed Commander of the new Space Force.

$$*\quad*\quad*\quad*\quad*$$

Merlynn...Faux Admissions Officer avatar at the Academy of Magic on Marinea (and former Queen Consort to King Scimitar).

Shamous...Owner of **Your Every Wish**, a magical shop on Marinea. New Crown Prince of Kronos, a Super Child/Twin of Rupert II.

Greta...Proprietor of Pro Bono shop, and a First Generation Super Child/Twin to Moonstone. Wed to Skye.

Vera...New Pro Bono lawyer in charge of interns.

Professor Yexer...Dissident at the Academy of Magic.

Trixie...Ringleader of older female magic students who 'acted out' at the Palace. Newly-discovered Queen-Designate of the kingdom of **Starlight** and First Generation Super Child. Super twin to Arkin. Now Recruitment Manager of the Space Force.

Arkin...Newly-identified First Generation Super Child and Marinean Ambassador Designate to Starlight. Super fraternal twin to Trixie.

Moonstone...Newly-identified First Generation Super Child and Twin to Greta. New Marinean Ambassador to Starlight.

Stefan...Fellow Graduate student and love interest of Andrea. Ambassador to Marinea from Planet X.

Dr. Hanover...Special Scientific Consultant to the Crown.

Alteria

Trident...Father of Tamara and Trina; wed to Terra; formerly a prince and King of Marinea; First Generation Super Child; Marinean Ambassador to Alteria.

Terra…Mother of Tamara and Trina; wed to Trident; also Head Watcher; undesignated Super Child.

Bugle…Terra's temporary replacement as Head Watcher while she is assigned elsewhere.

Tomas…Executive Assistant to Trident. Non-Magical Co-Leader of 'New Friends.'

Mimi…Magical co-leader of 'New Friends.'

Fern…A realtor from Alteria and friend of Terra.

Rose…Daughter of Queen Flora III of Timbere and Ambassador from Timbere to Alteria. First Generation Super Child/Twin to Merlynn. Wed to Georgio.

Violet…Executive Assistant to Rose.

New Space Force

(based on Alteria)

Georgio…Commander

Crystos…Second-in-Command

Trixie…Head of Recruitment

Andrea and **Leilani**…Trixie's original staff

Kert…Captain of Explorer 1

Patrik…Kert's Second in-Command and fraternal brother

Nolan…Captain of Explorer 2, then Explorer 4

Joy…Captain of Explorer 3

Dr. Jeen…Medical Doctor on Explorer 3

Mosshire

Sostor…An ice magic sorcerer on Mosshire; Ruler of the kingdom; a First Generation Super Child/Twin to Sunan of Mesarra; has fair skin, blonde hair and very blue eyes like residents of Mosshire. Wed to Solange, a Super Child/Sister to Savea.

Solange…Mother of Trident; Grandmother of Tamara and Trina; a First Generation Super Child/Twin to Savea. Wed to Sostor.

Coral and **Frosti**…Second Generation Super Sister/Twins/ Children of Solange and Sostor.

Pansy and Chrome…Watcher/Nannies to the twin girls of Solange and Sostor.

*   *   *   *   *

Rolf…Watcher and temporary ruler of Mosshire; and leader of an insurrection.

Trina…A First Generation Super Child and Sister/Twin to Queen Emerita Tamara. Wed to Jon. Marinean Ambassador to Mosshire. Now working in Academy President's Office.

Georgio…Interim Marinean Ambassador to Mosshire. (see Marinea for more complete description).

Mesarra

Sunan…A solar magic mage on Mesarra; Ruler of the kingdom; a First Generation Super Child/Twin to Sostor of Mosshire; has dark hair and eyes like residents of Mesarra. Wed to Merlynn.

Merlynn…Sunan's Assistant in establishing an Academy of Magic in Mesarra. A First Generation Super Child and Sister/Twin to Rose. Offered the position of Ambassador from Marinea to Mesarra by Queen Tamara. Wed to Sunan.

Trillium…A First Generation Super Child/Twin to Trident and Trident's identical twin; Marinean Ambassador to Mesarra. Reassigned as Marinean Ambassador to Starshine. Wed to Delia.

Delia…Trillium's first hire, the Embassy Manager on Mesarra. A First Generation Super Child. Wed to Trillium.

Carter…Delia's new Assistant.

Claud…Brief Prime Minister of Mesarra.

(On the dark side of Akura)

Primus

Forty…King of the kingdom of Primus (Personal name: **Linc**).

Martine…Member of Marinean Security Force; Marinean Ambassador to Primus.

Viktor…Commander-Designate of the new Seismic Alert Guard.

Aquelle

Scimitar…Former King of the kingdom of Aquelle; masqueraded as a rogue Watcher; sidekick of King Lucas of Brimstone. Now deceased.

Regis…Present Ruler and former Prime Minister of Aquelle.

Borel…Member of the Marinean Security Force; Marinean Ambassador to Aquelle.

Anna…Tour guide on Aquelle and first Executive Assistant to Borel.

Pieter…Second Executive Assistant to Borel.

Timbere

Flora III…Queen of the kingdom of Timbere; a First Generation Super Child and Sister/Twin to Queen Astrid of Seaside.

Rose…Daughter of Queen Flora III; a Second Generation Super Child/Twin to Merlynn. Timberean Ambassador to Alteria. Wed to Georgio.

Brooke…Secretary to Queen Flora.

Talia…Member of Marinean Security Force; Marinean Ambassador to Timbere.

Hazel...Executive Assistant to Talia.

Clark...Magical Co-Leader of the new experimental project in Timbere. Also a member of the Marinean Security Force. Temporary Ambassador to Alteria.

Borys...Non-magical Co-Leader of the new experimental project in Timbere.

Acorn... Owner of the tree-top restaurant.

Brimstone

Lucas...Former King of the kingdom of Brimstone. Wielder of shadow magic. Now deceased.

Lucian...Former government official and elected Ruler.

Scimitar...Former King of the kingdom of Aquelle; masqueraded as a rogue Watcher; sidekick of King Lucas. Now deceased.

Merlynn...True Admissions Officer of the Academy of Magic on Marinea; First Generation Super Child and Sister/Twin to Rose. Declared Queen Consort to King Scimitar at one point. The majority of her life was spent in captivity in Brimstone. Now helping Sunan establish an Academy of Magic in Mesarra. Granted Marinean citizenship by Queen Tamara and appointed as Marinean Ambassador to Mesarra. Wed to Sunan.

Exeter...Marinean Ambassador to Brimstone.

Angus...Once Ambassador-Designate to Farmview. Now Deputy Ambassador to Brimstone.

Freedom

(Name of the new island kingdom east of Brimstone, populated by refugees from Brimstone)

Cyril...Leader of the kingdom and First Generation Super Child/Twin brother of Cyrus. Wed to Candace of Marinea; Parents of Joy.

Cyrus…A First Generation Super Child/Twin brother of Cyril and Second-in-Command. Wed to Princess Sunny of Marinea.

Seaside

Astrid…Queen of the kingdom of Seaside; a First Generation Super Child and Sister/Twin of Queen Flora III of Timbere.

Kalia…Member of Marinean Security Force; Marinean Ambassador to Seaside.

Margo…Kalia's guide in Seaside.

Kronos

Rupert I…King of the Elven kingdom of Kronos, now deceased.

Rupert II…Present King of the Elven kingdom of Kronos, a First Generation Super Child/Twin of Shamous from Marinea.

Shamous…New Crown Prince of Kronos, a First Generation Super Child/Twin of Rupert II. Owner of **Your Every Wish**, a magical shop in Marinea.

Damon…Soldier and Tour Guide.

'Bu..bb..les'

Posidon…King of the undersea kingdom of 'Bu..bb..les.'

Shelley One…Daughter of King Posidon, a First Generation Super Child and Sister/Twin of Shelley Two.

Shelley Two…Daughter of King Posidon, a First Generation Super Child and Sister/Twin of Shelley One.

Dani…Marinean Ambassador to Bu..bb..les.

(On another astral plane)

The Crystal Castle

Adele and **Jeremy**…The Emeritus Super Beings.

Elsa…Watcher/Guardian at the Crystal Castle. Wed to Rogere.

Rogere…Watcher/Guardian at the Crystal Castle; Trident's biological father. Wed to Elsa.

Tamara and **Sean**…New Super Beings.

(Elsewhere in the Universe)

Starlight

An alien kingdom on the planet **Starbright.** Recently ruled by a King and Queen who were killed in a crash of their airship on Akura. Now succeeded by their daughter, **Trixie,** a Super Child living on the planet Akura. If officially crowned Queen, she will be known as **Queen Moonbeam,** after her mother.

Skort…Prime Minister of Starlight.

Arkin…Marinean Ambassador-Designate to Starlight; Super fraternal Twin to Trixie.

Beamie…Guide on Starlight who helped Arkin establish his Embassy.

Moonstone…New Marinean Ambassador to Starlight; First Generation Super Twin to Greta.

Neero…Leader of the Insurrectionists.

Shine…Embassy Chief-of-Staff.

Scotti…Manager of the Marinean Embassy Residence.

Trone…Leader of the Starlight Resistance.

Starshine

Another kingdom on the planet **Starbright.** (once known as Starlight). Ruled by Queen Bella, who had previously been imprisoned by the leaders of a military uprising and is now freed.

Bella…Queen of Starshine.

Malkum…Consort of the Queen.

Crystos…Originally appointed Marinean Ambassador to Starshine but reassigned as Second-in-Command of the Space Force; First Generation Super Child and Twin to Georgio. Upgraded by the Creator Being to remain a Fourth Generation being.

Trillium…A Super Child/Twin to Trident and Trident's identical twin; Marinean Ambassador to Mesarra. Reassigned as Marinean Ambassador to Starshine. Wed to Delia.

Former Planet X

(Now temporarily named 'Winner')

The Ruler…As yet unnamed.

Stefan…Ambassador from Planet X to Marinea.

Jaeda…Ambassador from Marinea to Planet X.

Thalia

A kingdom on the planet Divos on the other side of the galaxy. There is an active Resistance movement.

Nikos…the Ruler.

Kert…a refugee from Thalia who escaped through a Black Hole and reached Akura. Identified as a Super Child. Patrik's fraternal twin brother.

Patrik…a refugee from Thalia who escaped through a Black Hole and reached Akura. Identified as a Super Child. Kert's fraternal twin brother.

Dubbell

A kingdom on the planet Divos on the other side of the universe. Human residents are paired with avatars.

Ruler unnamed…Incarcerated by Security Force.

Unknown Planet G

Nolan… an alien who entered a Black Hole located on the far side of the universe reaching Akura via the arc of Time.

First Generation Super Children
(and their home kingdoms)

Female

Solange (Marinea/Mosshire) and **Savea** (Marinea)

Astrid (Seaside) and **Flora** (Timbere)

Rose (Timbere) and **Merlynn** (Brimstone/Marinea)

Tamara (Alteria/Marinea) and **Trina** (Alteria/Marinea)

Shelley One and **Shelley Two** (Bu..bb..les)

Trixie (Marinea/Starlight) and **Arkin** (male, Marinea/ Starlight)

Greta (Marinea) and **Moonstone** (Marinea and Starlight)

Male

Sostor (Mosshire) and **Sunan** (Mesarra)

Sean (Marinea) and **Jon** (Marinea)

Trident (Marinea) and **Trillium** (Marinea)

Cyril (Brimstone/Freedom) and **Cyrus** (Brimstone/Freedom)

Rupert II (Kronos) and **Shamous** (Marinea/Kronos)

Arkin (Marinea/Starlight) and **Trixie** (female, Marinea/ Starlight)

Georgio (Marinea) and **Crystos** (Marinea)

Second Generation Super Children
(Marinea)

Candace…Queen of Marinea and Daughter of Queen Emerita Tamara and Commander Emeritus Sean. An original Super Child. Wed to Cyril.

Skye…Prince and Son of Queen Emerita Tamara and Commander Emeritus Sean. An original Super Child. Wed to Greta.

Sunny…Princess and Daughter of Queen Emerita Tamara and Commander Emeritus Sean. An original Super Child. Wed to Cyrus.

Verd…Prince and Son of Queen Emerita Tamara and Commander Emeritus Sean. An original Super Child. Wed to Savea; father of Lavan and Wavan.

Tristan and **Brendan**…the Second Generation twin sons of Trina and Jon.

Savea…Upgraded after being wed to Verd.

Cyril…Upgraded after being wed to Candace.

Cyrus…Upgraded after being wed to Sunny.

(Mosshire)

Coral and **Frosti**…Second Generation Super Sisters Twins/ Children of Solange and Sostor.

Third Generation Super Children
(Marinea)

Lavan and **Wavan**…Super Twins/Brothers; children of Savea and Verd.

Fourth Generation Super Children
(Marinea)

Leilani and **Andrea**…the twin daughters of Tamara and Sean.

Crystos. . . Upgraded to Fourth Generation by the Creator Being.

Kert and **Patrik**…Upgraded to Fourth Generation by Creator Being.

Sixth Generation Super Children (Marinea/Freedom)

Joy…First-born daughter of Candace and Cyril. New Queen-Designate.

Nolan…Upgraded by Creator Being.

Eighth Generation Super Children (Marinea)

Savior (Savvy)…First-born of Joy and Nolan

Tenth Generation Super Children (Marinea)

Starr. . .Second-born of Joy and Nolan

Twelfth Generation Super Children (Marinea)

Scarlett and Pepper…New fraternal twins of Queen Emerita Tamara and Commander Emeritus Sean Lockette

Fernne and **Forrest**…New fraternal twins of Queen Candace and Consort Cecil.

---

*The Creator Being has a policy of upgrading so that both wedded parties are the same generation.

Crystal Saga Series 4

1 — Defense = Offense

D. E. Weingand

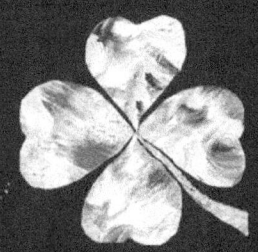

Prologue

My name is Nolan. My home planet is on the other side of the universe. I had no memories of childhood until I found myself walking alone through the streets of an unfamiliar city—which turned out to be in the undersea kingdom of Marinea on the planet of Akura.

When I stumbled into the Academy of Magic and told the professors my story, everyone got very excited. It turned out that I was a Super Child and it was common to not remember anything until puberty. Once they pronounced me a Super Child, my memories began to return.

There was a lot of strife on my home planet and members of the Resistance had adopted me. As I grew older, I began to understand what they wanted—and that they intended to use violence to get it. So, one day, I stole a small rocket ship and aimed it at the nearby Black Hole, hoping I would emerge in a better place. I was lucky, because I did.

However, members of the Resistance followed me through the Black Hole and have been hunting me ever since. I managed to evade them for years, as I attended classes in the Academy. Once I graduated, though, and joined the Security Force, I guess

I became more visible—and they have been hounding me to return to my home planet, which I didn't want to do.

When the Space Force was established, I transferred to join it and rapidly advanced through the ranks. I had always been a good student at the Academy and had studied management there, with an emphasis on leadership. I was surprised—and grateful—when I was offered the post of Captain of Explorer 2.

I think my new position threatened those who were shadowing me because there began to be attempts on my life. I was able to avoid them, but then I found Joy. We had been students at the Academy together and I had accompanied her on a few of her Time travel adventures.

But there came a day when our paths crossed more intensely and Joy told me that we had been identified as 'true mates'. I didn't know what that meant, but I soon learned. Joy explained to me that the power surge which occurred when our hands touched was the signal that we were 'true mates'. She had asked her great-grandmother, Terra, to confirm it—which she did.

We have recently been wed, along with three other couples from the Space Force (who were also 'true mates'). Sadly, the threats and attempts on my life increased and when we took Explorer 2 out for a training mission, it became critical. Fortunately, Joy had insisted on coming with me and she was able to temporarily save our Ship. Our crew was replaced with avatars by the Creator Being; they would perish when the Ship was destroyed. Our human crew will have a secure future now outside of the Space Force and a new crew will be assigned before our next mission.

I said that Joy saved us, but that is not quite accurate. Joy and I didn't know that she was with child, and it was our child that saved us both. Our daughter had not as yet been born, yet she was able to teleport us back to Base. She is a true miracle. We named her Savior, and lovingly call her Savvy.

Savvy, like her mother, was impatient and wanted to accelerate her growth. She did so and was able to attend the party that she and Joy had planned. That party was interrupted by an altercation with what I thought was another Resistance fighter from my home planet.

Sean was able to capture and interrogate him. The end of that story has not yet been written. My mate and daughter are my life; I would do anything to protect them.

Chapter 1
The Meeting

Sean had decided to use the Space Force auditorium for the meeting of both Forces and the Super Children from around the planet. Although he had made attendance mandatory, he rather doubted that this requirement had been necessary.

The auditorium filled up quickly. When Sean reached the podium, he began by giving a summary of Nolan's background. Looking over the audience, he could see the shock passing across most of the faces. Once the shock reaction had abated, he moved on to describe the aliens who had followed Nolan through the faraway Black Hole—emphasizing that they were thought to be Resistance members with an agenda that included violence.

As Scan beckoned Nolan to the podium, he could see a wave of unease pass through the audience. However, Nolan's leadership skills—enhanced by Sean's calming spell—restored order.

Nolan had decided to revisit Sean's presentation in his own comments. He brought a personal interpretation to what they had already heard—a personal recount of being an alien on a foreign planet who had no memory and was actually fleeing for his life.

He proceeded to paint a picture of being welcomed by the Academy, being identified as a Super Child, and rising in the ranks because of his own capabilities. Then he switched to darker intel.

As he related his awareness that he was being followed on many occasions, a murmuring arose in the audience. Nolan switched to providing details of the capture of alien dissidents and their present status.

Sean moved next to Nolan and invited comments from the audience. There were many questions asked and answered. When the frequency of input lessened, Sean shifted into a problem-solving mode.

"Some of my staff are passing out a document that requests ideas for moving forward. The aliens that we have in custody have admitted to an invasion agenda—which we obviously must take seriously as we plan our defense strategies. On the document also is a way for you to volunteer personally to defend our planet. Commander Georgio and I will work together to mount the strongest defense possible...and we welcome your involvement.

"I must emphasize that the clock is ticking. We do not know when an invasion will arrive, but we believe that it is imminent. So, as you process what you have heard today, please keep that caution in your mind. Dismissed."

*　　*　　*　　*　　*

Georgio led Sean and Nolan back to his office. The planning for defending Akura was about to begin.

"I found the presentation to be both clear and comprehensive," Georgio began. "Nolan, I think you were able to defuse the initial fear by personalizing your experience. That was very effective."

"Thank you, Sir," responded Nolan. "But I need to insist that Joy be present at these planning meetings. She has already been promoted to Captain of Explorer 3. I would be fine serving under her command. In fact, I have already done so during our defense against the ships of the known hostile planet within their Black Hole.

"I need to stress that we are facing two hostile planets. I don't know the location of my birth planet at this time. We must first deal with the one before us.

"My personal recommendation is that the best defense is a good offense. I think we should take a cloaked Explorer 3 into our own Black Hole—since we know it can be a conduit. We can land in a remote area of the known hostile planet   or orbit the planet— sending a group of Force members on an Astral Journey to gather intelligence."

"That's an interesting idea," approved Sean. "Before we do that, however, I want to question the prisoners again to determine what, if any, magical abilities are present in the population."

"An important point, Sean," Georgio agreed. "Simply cloaking the Ship and Force members would be insufficient if they can be detected in some manner."

"Very true," Nolan said. "May I send for Joy now, Sir? I'm not comfortable proceeding any further without her."

"Of course," Georgio approved. "And thank you for pointing out the importance of her presence." Nolan sent a mental message to Joy and there was a knock at the door.

"I've been waiting to be invited, Sir," smiled Joy, who was carrying Savvy. "I want to add one more important point to your conversation. We need to begin a rush project of producing Ships. We really should prepare an armada to be at the ready. I have seen that we do so."

The two Commanders looked at each other and grinned. They would never dispute what Joy claimed to have seen.

*   *   *   *   *

Joy and Nolan took turns carrying Savvy on the way home. She was growing so fast that, even though she was still considered a babe, her skill set was more that of a child about to enter school! "Why did Commander Georgio want Savvy to be at today's meeting?" asked Joy.

"I'm not sure," admitted Nolan. "He said he had a feeling that she would be needed. That's all I know."

Savvy wiggled a little in her mother's arms—and winked at her father.

Chapter 2
Explorer 3

Georgio authorized a speeded-up construction schedule for as many new Ships as could be possible at the present time. As each Ship was completed, another one would be added to the schedule.

Since Nolan had been Captain of the destroyed Explorer 2 and now would be Captain of Explorer 4, he would be overseeing its construction. Joy, already designated the Captain of Explorer 3, continued to monitor its completion.

Savvy was interested in both Ships' progress and loved to accompany her parents during inspection visits. She kept the mental connection with her mother; vocal speech was not as yet one of her abilities...but Joy sensed that it wasn't far off. Whenever Savvy had a comment about her father's Ship, she asked her mother to transmit it to him.

One day, Savvy tired of using her mother as an intermediary and decided to speak. Her voice was soft and musical, but the volume could be intensified easily. Joy was delighted that her babe would now be communicating personally instead of using her as a translator.

*   *   *   *   *

It was time to christen Explorer 3. As Captain of that vessel, Joy was allowed to do the honors—especially since the Ship she had once christened was no longer in existence. She climbed the stairs to the platform. Once she was there, she felt Savvy teleport into her arms. Apparently, Savvy wanted to be part of 'the action.'

Joy grabbed the bottle of bubbly and pulled it back, preparing to let it fly against the hull of Explorer 3. Suddenly she was aware that Savvy's hand was on top of hers—and the bottle soared toward the Ship. Savvy yelled, "We christen you Explorer 3!"

All the spectators began to laugh and clap. Savvy looked around proudly, smiling and waving. Joy gazed at Nolan, who was standing behind her, "I think our wee one has a streak of showpersonship!"

Nolan nodded and reached for Savvy. "I agree," he said. With his free hand, he clasped Joy's and the three of them descended to the ground. "I plan to ask Andrea if she would do the honors for Explorer 4—but I'll need to warn her that she may have an unexpected assistant!"

"That would be wise, Dear," Joy giggled and they began to walk home. Savvy kissed her father on the cheek and teleported to the ground. She started skipping in front of them as they watched her latest skill.

"Life is never dull with Savvy around, is it?" commented Nolan.

"No," agreed Joy. "It's impossible to predict what she will do next. I definitely support Sean's decision to allow her on board our Ships. In my Time travels, I haven't seen her in action—but I believe she will play an important role."

*   *   *   *   *

Explorer 3 was on the launching pad, ready to lift off on her first training mission. Joy and Savvy were standing at the Ship's entrance, ready to board. Nolan had decided to join them on the mission after giving detailed instructions to the workers who were diligently trying to complete Explorer 4's construction in record time. By the time Explorer 3 returned to Base, Explorer 4 would be ready to be christened.

*   *   *   *   *

The training mission was proceeding without incident, during which time Savvy had continually roamed around, absorbing intel about the Ship's operations. The crew had observed her inspections with interest, but soon became used to seeing her, focusing on their own duties.

As Savvy passed the Communications and Pilot stations, she suddenly stopped. She had learned that Explorer 2 was sabotaged at these two points and gave them some special attention.

Her blue eyes changed color and a green beam surged toward the two suspect stations. She immediately noticed that some wires had been cut—and proceeded to reconnect them. Her parents observed what she was doing with amazement, thankful that they had listened to Sean's advice.

When the repair had been completed, Joy sent an urgent message back to Base, informing Georgio and Crystos of the almost fatal sabotage that Savvy had discovered and corrected. She urged them to immediately quarantine all Ground Crew who had worked on the Ship prior to lift-off and ask Sean to interrogate them.

"How did you know there would be a problem?" Nolan asked Savvy.

"I knew what had happened before," replied Savvy, "so I decided to give those stations some extra attention."

"I'm very glad your instincts were so accurate," praised Joy. "Thank you. What was that green beam that you used?"

"A combination of x-ray and various beams that could reconnect elements of the Ship. I felt sure that there would be another attempt," Savvy insisted. "My intuitive skills are pretty strong."

Nolan knelt before his daughter and held her hands. "You

are our secret weapon, Savvy. Your official name is Savior—and you definitely just saved us. You are welcome on our Ships whenever you wish to be there."

Joy whispered to Nolan, "And, if my eyes don't deceive me, I think she has grown several inches taller since we left Base."

Nolan nodded agreement and Joy gave the order to return to Base.

Chapter 3
Investigating Sabotage

Sean was not surprised when he received the urgent summons from Georgio. Hurrying to the Space Force Base, he was thoroughly briefed about Joy's message. Crystos had already sequestered the Ground Crew members who had worked on Explorer 3.

It was a large group of Space Force staff who had been granted access to the Ship. This would be a long and complex interrogation effort. Sean sighed and wondered whether Savvy could be helpful to him. He would ask as soon as the Ship returned to Base.

One thing was certain: the aliens he had already interrogated were still in custody. That meant that they could not have personally done the sabotage. However, he would check the visitor rolls to see what contacts they had received while incarcerated.

*   *   *   *   *

Hearing that Explorer 3 had landed, he rushed to greet Joy, Nolan and Savvy. On the way, he gathered a large number of Space Force members. Ordering them to detain the entire crew for questioning, he approached the Ship and waved to Captain Joy and her family. He blinked when he looked at Savvy; she was definitely taller than when he had last seen her. which wasn't that long ago.

He walked up to Savvy and looked her in the face. Commenting on her apparent growth, he observed the twinkle in her eye. Savvy smiled and admitted that she had boosted her development again in order to be of more help on the training mission.

Sean took her hand and asked whether she would be able to be of assistance in the multiple interrogations that needed to be done. She nodded and agreed to work with him. "It won't take long, Grandpapa. I'll be able to tell right away which ones to question."

Sean was relieved to hear her response, but wondered how it could work. He wanted to start with the Ship's crew so they could continue their onboard duties, and Savvy agreed.

Sean and Savvy boarded Explorer 3 and Savvy walked over to each crew member, touching their face as she did so. When she had finished, she reported that no one of the Explorer 3 crew had been involved.

"Are you certain?" asked Sean hesitantly.

"Yes, Grandpapa," she replied. "Can I call you Papa? I can

tell right away if someone is telling the truth. It's one of my Eighth Generation abilities. Who should we test now?"

Sean shook his head; he had a hard time understanding Savvy's pronouncement. "Let's move over to Ground Control and check them out," he said.

Savvy repeated her process in the Ground Control building, but the results were different. She identified several staff members as being complicit in the attempted sabotage. Sean had them taken to the Security Force detention center for further questioning.

Sean, Savvy and her parents teleported to Security Force Headquarters in order to continue the investigation. While there, he asked for a list of visitors to the already detained aliens and received a lengthy report. Apparently, there had been several visitors who had made repeated appearances. This was beginning to look like a serious security issue.

He gave the order to detain any future visitors. At that moment, the same ones showed up and were arrested. He had them put into the same cell as the original prisoners.

"Papa," asked Savvy, "do you want me to make them tell you the truth?"

"You can do that?" he inquired.

"Of course," she smiled. She cast a white haze into the cell in front of them that covered all the prisoners inside. "Ask them anything now."

Sean began his normal interrogation technique and, one by one, they answered him truthfully, confirmed by the vid screen over their heads. It turned out that the visitors were also from the aliens' home planet. They were a communications link between the planet and the prisoners that had been captured so far.

He learned that the Ground Control suspects had been subject to a form of mind control performed by these visitors and were unwilling victims. He asked Savvy if there was a way to cleanse their minds of the alien interference and she agreed to do so.

Moving over to the cell containing the Ground Control detainees, she cast a pink haze that engulfed them totally. They held their heads and Sean watched smoke emerge from their ears. When it had dissipated, Savvy told him that they would no longer remember anything that they had done to the Ship.

Sean returned to the visitors' cell and proceeded to ask questions about their planet and how many spies were on Akura. He was appalled to find out how many spies were already on Akura, having come through the Black Hole on the near side of the galaxy. The invasion had already begun—and it was a very subtle one.

Chapter 4
Avatars?

Tamara declared a State of Emergency. A Council of War was formed, with members from both Marinea and Alteria. Additional detention cells were built on Marinea to hold the spies that had been located already—plus the ones yet to be discovered.

Joy and Nolan were frustrated; they were merely observers as their daughter created miracles to help Joy's grandfather. Finally, they approached her and asked how they could be involved.

Savvy looked at them quizzically and asked her mother if there was any way to surround the entire planet with a cleansing haze—one that would capture or eliminate every spy.

Sean turned and admitted to overhearing their conversation. "Do you know if these spies are human or avatars?"

Joy answered, "I believe they are avatars, Grandpa…at least, they behave like them. Why do you ask? Does it make a difference?"

"Absolutely," Sean responded happily. "Some time ago, we had difficulties with avatars and created a way to make them self-destruct. I'll contact Sunan and ask him to come here. My memory is a bit fuzzy about how we did it—but I'm sure he'll remember."

*   *   *   *   *

Sunan arrived the following day. When Sean explained why he had been summoned, Sunan smiled. "I had a feeling that you might need me sometime in the future."

Sean commented, "That future is now. While we were successful in eliminating avatars on Akura, we have encountered them on other planets. Nolan and Joy are speculating that the spies from the other end of the Black Hole might possibly be avatars. If so, we need to replicate your self-destruct method."

"Sounds like a reasonable request," Sunan asserted. "Where are your detainees now?"

"In the Security Force Detention Center," said Sean. Taking Sunan's arm, he teleported them to that location.

Joy, Nolan and Savvy were waiting for them. Savvy had been busy soliciting truthful responses from the spies. "Papa," she began, "I have been able to ascertain the truth from all of the spies. Every one is an avatar that is a replica of a human still living on their planet."

Sunan looked at Sean and told him to bring two of the spies to an empty cell. Sean complied and did so, casting a spell to immobilize them upon their arrival in the cell. Sunan waved his hand and produced the necessary surgical implements he would need. Proceeding to surgically expose the AI opening beneath their mouths that led to the AI brains, he saw that the connections had already been created.

After reassembling the avatars, he was ready to speak the trigger phrase 'Do it now!' that would initiate the self-destruct mechanism. Before doing so, he needed to confirm with Sean that he had already secured the necessary intel.

Sean turned to Joy and asked whether they had all they needed. She nodded and he gave Sunan the go-ahead to begin the trigger phrase. "Do it now!" Sunan shouted. As they all watched, the two avatars began to smoke and soon were piles of ash. In the other cells, all avatars followed the same pattern.

Reports began to come in from other locations on Akura that similar results were occurring with previously unknown avatars.

"I think your immediate problem has been solved," commented Sunan. "However, you need to be on the alert for other avatars coming through the Black Holes."

"Is there any way we can identify new avatars who might appear?" asked Sean.

Savvy piped up, "I'll know, Papa. I'll point them out for you."

Bending over, Sean thanked Savvy for her efforts and promised to make sure she would be on Explorer 3 when it lifted off. Sunan watched with amusement.

"Your Space Force is recruiting new members that are quite young," Sunan observed.

"I'm Eighth Generation," boasted Savvy. "I have special skills that my parents believe will be helpful."

"How old are you?" Sunan asked Savvy.

"I'm not sure," she replied. "I think I look much older than my real age. I've speeded up my development."

"Really?" exclaimed Sunan. "How did you do that?"

"My mother did it, too," confessed Savvy "and I learned how from her."

Sunan looked at Joy with astonishment. "Is that true? How is it possible?"

Joy blushed and admitted that it was definitely true...It was part of her Sixth Generation set of abilities—and Savvy was able to take it to the next level.

"And what is the next level?" pressed Sunan.

"She can do it faster and more completely than I could," replied Joy. "As to the extent of her Eighth Generation talents...

we really don't know. We watch and record her actions, but there seems to be something new every day."

Sunan shook his head in consternation. There was so much to absorb...and his world seems to be changing so fast! Accelerated growth! A babe who is fighting battles—and winning! He used to feel that he was in control of his kingdom and understood challenges as they appeared. Now he wasn't so sure!

Sending a mental message to Sean, he entreated him to share new developments as they occurred. Sean nodded and embraced his good friend, who then vanished.

Sean returned to his office and pondered what had just taken place with the avatars. He decided to find Georgio to do some needed strategizing.

Chapter 5
Good Defense = Offense

Sean teleported to a spot just outside Georgio's office door.

Knocking softly, he stepped inside when invited. Taking a seat, he brought Georgio up-to-date on the avatar situation.

Georgio leaned back in his chair and wiped his brow. "So tell me if I understand this correctly," he requested. "The perpetrators were actually avatars of actual beings from a hostile kingdom or planet. After you interrogated them, you sent for Sunan because the two of you had once worked together to rid our planet of all avatars by initiating an effective self-destruct mechanism. Do I have it right?"

"Yes," affirmed Sean. "And after watching Savvy use some of her powers, he teleported home scratching his head!"

"No doubt!" laughed Georgio. "It sounds to me like we are in the midst of a serious situation with that planet—what's its name, by the way?"

"I don't know," admitted Sean. "But this latest victory over the known avatars on Akura feels like just the opening skirmish.

We need to come up with a defense plan and present it to Tamara's Council of War."

"I agree," responded Georgio. "I propose that we form our own Defense Team, composed of our Ship Captains, Crystos, you and me. Do you concur?"

"I think that would be a good first step," Sean replied, "but I believe we need to think much more broadly. For example, at some point I suspect that we will need to enter our Black Hole and make our defense into an offensive move to eradicate all avatars on that planet. That said, I'd like Sunan to be appointed to the Team as well."

"Eradication would be a bold move," approved Georgio. "However, I think some diplomatic relations should be tried before doing so. I'll call a meeting of our Defense Team for tomorrow and we can begin brainstorming. I will invite Sunan, as you suggest."

*   *   *   *   *

The next day, the newly-formed Defense Team gathered in the conference room adjacent to Georgio's office. Georgio noticed that Joy and Nolan had brought Savvy along with them.

Sean and Sunan briefed the Team about the self-destruction of the avatars. They also introduced the idea that a similar effort may well be necessary in the future.

Brainstorming continued through the day, but no definitive strategies were established. A meeting was scheduled for the next day, with a preliminary report to be created and submitted to the Council of War.

Before disbanding for the day, Sean made a proposal to be put on the next day's agenda. "When my kingdom of Marinea decided to pursue diplomacy, I created birds to transmit messages. I suggest sending birds through the Black Hole with similar messages—and see what happens."

There was a general murmur of approval and Georgio agreed to put it up for discussion the next day.

*   *   *   *   *

At the next meeting, Sean's proposal was unanimously approved. Next on the agenda was a proposal from Georgio. He suggested that the two in-service Ships, Explorers 1 and 3, be sent on training flights, ending in a mission of observing the known Black Holes. Until other Ships could be completed and deployed, they would monitor the Black Holes to make sure no hostile entities emerged. Both Ships would deliver Sean's new birds to the near Black Hole and dispatch them. Then it would be a waiting game. The far Black Hole had been sealed.

When all agenda items had been discussed, the two Commanders and Sunan teleported over to Marinea to meet with the Council of War. Since the Council was now composed of both military and civilian members from kingdoms around the planet, they would need to communicate in very clear language, avoiding all jargon. It would be a definite challenge.

This would be a new experience for the three representatives of the Defense Team. Since any decisions would affect the entire planet, clear communication and diplomacy would be absolutely required.

Sean knocked on the Palace conference room door and they entered. Tamara stood and welcomed them warmly. This meeting would be a 'first' of its kind on Akura. Another change in how the kingdoms would interact in the near future.

Tamara called the meeting to order.

Chapter 6
Learning New Ways

Since the meeting was occurring in Marinea, Sean spoke first, as Commander of the Security Force. He described in detail the events that had occurred and their belief that the perpetrators were avatars—a belief that had been proven to be true.

He then asked Sunan to summarize their shared background on Akura and their successful termination of the avatars planet-wide. Sunan continued his remarks by telling the Council that Sean had requested his help with the current prisoners who were assumed to be avatars.

After replicating the conditions used in his prior encounter with avatars, the results were the same: avatars had self-destructed planet-wide in the same way that had happened previously.

Sean and Sunan were peppered with questions, which they handled easily. When the frequency slowed, Sean took control again and reminded the Council that the danger was still present. He then turned the meeting over to Georgio, Commander of the Space Force.

Georgio thanked Sean and Sunan for combining their experience and skills for another successful result with the avatars on Akura. However, he stressed that additional invasions using one or more Black Holes were still possible.

Sharing the Defense Team's recent recommendation to monitor the Black Holes, he stopped short of relating any details about how that would be accomplished. Citing security considerations, he asked for the Council's trust that such a mission was already being put into motion.

The Council clapped approval and praised the report they had just received. They looked relieved that military experts appeared to have the situation well-in-hand.

Tamara stood and addressed the Council. "Like you, I am very satisfied with the direction that the Defense Team has charted. I would therefore propose that this Council rename itself and its purpose. Since the membership of the Council now includes representation from all the kingdoms of Akura, I suggest that its purpose be expanded beyond war, encompassing all issues that face us on this planet. We could revise its name to be the Council of Kingdoms and rewrite its charter to reflect its new mission."

The delegates stood and called for a vote to support Tamara's recommendation. An immediate vote was taken…and it was unanimous. The next step would be to nominate candidates for the position of General Manager. One moon's time would be given for potential names to be nominated; an election would take place at that time.

Tamara thanked the Council delegates for their service and the representatives from the Defense Team for their presentations. She dismissed the Council and invited everyone into the Garden for refreshments.

*   *   *   *   *

Tamara and Sean found a vacant bench after doing their political duties interacting with Council members in the Garden. Refreshments had been very welcome and served as a pleasant conclusion to the day. Tamara leaned into Sean's shoulder and sighed.

"Sean, thank you for that very informative presentation," she began. "Bringing Sunan along was a master stroke. He has a very calming demeanor and the Council delegates seemed very impressed."

"Thank you," Sean replied. "Be sure to tell him yourself. He's coming toward us now."

As Sunan approached, Tamara and Sean stood, Tamara greeting him warmly, expressing her thanks personally. They chatted briefly about the meeting and then Sunan changed the topic to Tamara's proposal for changing the Council's mission to a broader context.

"I applaud your vision," praised Sunan. "I think our planet has grown so much from its early beginnings with diplomacy. But I'm intrigued that Sean's birds will still have a role."

"Sometimes a simple technology continues to have value," commented Sean. "I'm more comfortable using the birds as a first effort to connect with Planet A for Avatar, rather than just sending our Spaceships into the Hole. However, I don't rule that approach out, depending on Planet A's response to the birds."

"You were wise not to share defense details with such a large audience, Sean," pressed Sunan. "As the Ruler of one of Akura's kingdoms, I definitely recommend keeping the Council a diplomatic entity with limited access to military planning."

Tamara nodded her approval. "I remember when Marinea was the totality of my sphere of interest and responsibility. Then the concept of diplomatic relationships expanded my thinking into a world view.

"Now we have before us a huge jump from global concerns to galaxy-wide opportunities and threats. No wonder my head hurts!"

"Rest easy, Your Majesty," Sunan said in a soothing voice. "You have the support of many and, so far, you are anticipating issues that are yet to emerge. We can hope that potential inter-galactic opportunities will outweigh any as yet unknown threats."

Bowing, Sunan vanished.

Sean put his arm around Tamara's now trembling shoulders, reminding her, "There was a time when Sunan himself was a threat. Now he is a staunch supporter. You have done so much to make our kingdom and our planet safe and secure. Hold those memories close when you are feeling insecure or worried."

Tamara smiled up at her mate gratefully and sighed. "You are my rock and number one supporter, Dear. Whatever success I have had is yours to share." This tender moment was sealed with a loving kiss.

Chapter 7
More Training Missions

The Captains of Explorers 1 and 3, Kert and Joy, were readying their crews for a combined training mission. Kert was working closely with his Second-in-Command, Patrik.

Joy had yet to appoint hers and was hoping that one of the crew would stand out during this training mission. Temporarily, she had asked Nolan, her mate and the former Captain of the destroyed Explorer 2, to assume that position.

Nolan was presently the Captain-Designate of Explorer 4, which was still under expedited construction. His duties on Explorer 3 were unusual and beyond any professional job description: he would be also engaged in his parental role, supervising his daughter, Savvy.

Savvy was very excited to be allowed to be part of the crew on Explorer 3. Commander Georgio had specifically authorized this unusual deployment.

She walked purposefully around the Control Room, double-checking instruments and familiarizing herself with all the crew. As she approached her mother, she stopped moving and stood very still. Smiling, she walked up to Joy and touched her uniform.

"Mama," Savvy began, "I have discovered an unauthorized being aboard our Ship."

Joy turned abruptly and asked Savvy, "Where is this being and how did you discover its presence?"

Savvy giggled and patted her mother's tummy. "He just started talking to me, Mama, just like I began talking to you before I was born."

Nolan noticed that Joy's face had grown pale and hurried over. "Is something the matter, Dear?"

"I guess that depends upon one's point-of-view," Joy replied, reaching back to her Command Chair to sit down. "Our daughter has just informed me that she and HER BROTHER have started to communicate!

"How did I not know this, Savvy?" Joy asked her daughter.

"He said he wanted me to teach him how to talk to you…and I agreed, of course," Savvy continued, "You'll be hearing from him soon. But can we give him a name? I hated being referred to as 'the babe'."

Nolan retreated to his official chair and wiped his brow. "Since your mother and I have important duties to attend to, Savvy, why don't you bring us a list of possible names that your brother approves of. But first, would you please ask the Ship's doctor to come to the Control Room?"

Savvy hurried away to fulfill that request and Nolan turned to Joy. "Did you have any idea of what she just told us?"

"Absolutely not," Joy sighed. "The timing is terrible. And I just received his first try at talking to me." She grew silent as she internally responded to her son.

"I welcomed him to our family," she said, smiling at Nolan. "And I asked him to talk primarily to Savvy while our Ship is in flight. I simply cannot have the distraction."

"It seems that Savvy's presence will be doubly useful on this flight," agreed Nolan. "Please let me know if you need or want anything, Joy. I want to be as helpful as possible."

At that moment, Savvy returned with Dr. Jeen, the onboard physician. "How soon is lift-off, Captain?" she asked Joy.

Joy replied, "Two hours."

"Good, then we have time to go to Sick Bay for a quick check-up," the doctor proposed. Taking Joy's arm, she led her away.

"Don't worry, Da," assured Savvy. "Mama will be fine. I already examined her...and my brother is very healthy. By the way, he likes the name Starr."

"Thank you for that," Nolan said as he hugged her. "And why are you calling me 'Da'?"

"Grandma calls her father 'Da'," she answered, "and I liked the sound of it. Is it OK?" she asked.

"Of course, Darling," Nolan accepted as he hugged Savvy again. "You can call me anything you wish. I was just curious."

Nolan assumed the Captain's chair and sighed. This was going to be a very different kind of training mission!

*   *   *   *   *

With one hour to spare, Joy returned to the Control Room. She had been cleared for duty by the Ship's doctor and walked over to the Command Chair, which Nolan vacated as soon as he saw her approach.

"I've been cleared by Dr. Jeen," she reported.

"I had no doubts," smiled Nolan. "Our daughter already informed me that both you and Starr are healthy."

"Starr?" inquired Joy.

"She also let me know that our son prefers that name."

Sighing, Joy commented, "This is quite a novel start to a training mission."

"I definitely agree," laughed Nolan. "But we've had strange adventures before on our arc of Time journeys. "And I need to ask:

Why didn't you foresee this on one of your Time travels?"

"I've wondered that myself," admitted Joy. "Then I remembered that I haven't taken one since we began planning our wedding. Pardon the pun, but there hasn't been time!"

"That makes sense," agreed Nolan. "It seems that our son has a time sense of his own. I wonder what powers he will have—and what Generation he will be. Here's a pun of my own: time will tell!"

Groaning, Joy ordered the countdown to lift-off to begin.

Chapter 8
The Training Mission

Explorer 3 lifted off right on schedule. Explorer 1 had already departed. The two Ships were to meet a safe distance from the far Black Hole. Joy hoped that the Journey would be uneventful. She had enough on her mind today.

When they were successfully underway, she invited Savvy to come to her Command Chair.

"I need some intel from you, Dear," she began. "How did you know that Starr and I were healthy? That is what you told your father, isn't it?"

"Yes, Mama," Savvy answered. "It's one of my Eighth Generation abilities. I can sense good or ill health and also injury. Da was so worried and I wanted to make him feel better."

"And you knew I was with child because Starr began communicating with you?"

"Yes," Savvy responded. "I was walking around the Control Room, checking on the instruments, when I felt his first attempt. I stopped walking and focused on the source of the communication. That's when I located it inside your tummy."

"That's amazing, Dear," praised Joy. "Are the two of you still communicating?"

"Oh yes," Savvy exclaimed, "He's quite fascinated with being able to reach me."

"After his first message to me," Joy continued, "I asked him to talk only to you until I had this Ship safely back at Base. Since I've heard nothing further from him, can I assume that he is still in contact with you?"

"He is, Mama," giggled Savvy, "although I've had to tutor him in what a Spaceship is, and how important a training mission can be. He seems to grasp things quite quickly. In fact, he's quite impressed that his mother is the Captain…and he wants to be one someday!"

"Oh my!" exclaimed Joy. "I think you had better prepare yourself. I think Starr may well make demands upon both of us once he is born! Did he show any inclination to speed up his growth the way you and I have done?"

"He's already asking questions, Mama," Savvy admitted. "Is it OK for me to respond truthfully?"

"Of course," Joy emphasized. "Truth is always important. But please share both his questions and your answers with me until Starr and I are back in communication. Are you fine with that?"

"Yes, Mama…unless it's a private talk. And I'll let you know when it is."

"One more thing…" continued Joy. "What you are sharing with me sounds pretty advanced. Do you think Starr is already accelerating his growth?"

"I suspect that he is," replied Savvy. "His questions are pretty sophisticated—and becoming more so. I'm going to ask him to be sure he isn't born before we're back home…and hope he listens!"

Joy blanched. "Surely he doesn't have that much power."

"I believe that he does, Mama," Savvy said intensely. "I'll do my best to slow him down."

*   *   *   *   *

The two Ships reached their meeting point right on schedule. Their journeys had been uneventful and the training had been very successful. Captain Kert and Patrik teleported over to the Bridge of Explorer 3 to meet with Captains Joy and Nolan.

Joy escorted them to her Ready Room for a private conversation. In the spirit of complete transparency, she informed them about Starr and her instructions to him. The look of shock on their faces was quite amusing, she thought—just before she let them know that her daughter, Savvy, was in communication with Starr.

Captain Kert hesitantly asked Joy if she felt she should recuse herself until after giving birth. She smiled. stressing that she had no intention of doing so—reminding him that her Sixth Generation status provided many benefits, both personally and for the Ship.

He apologized for being insensitive, acknowledging the truth of her remarks, and promised to be more professional in the future.

Their discussion returned to the original agenda, which included a list of combined training activities while both Ships were situated near the far Black Hole. Although the far Black Hole had been sealed, cautious monitoring was indicated in case the enemy had discovered how to open it again. Some of that training involved taking action if hostile actors appeared coming from the Black Hole. They practiced intricate types of maneuvering, designed to confuse the enemy and protect each other.

When both Captains were satisfied with the results of the training, they drew lots to see which Ship would remain by this Black Hole and which Ship would head back to hover by the Black

Hole nearest the portion of the Galaxy they called home.

Joy was secretly relieved that Explorer 3 would be homeward bound, leaving Explorer 1 to monitor the far Black Hole. She wasn't sure how far her teleportation skills extended—and it was comforting to know that they would be adequate near the Black Hole closest to home.

As she turned the Command over to Nolan to grab some needed sleep, she decided to break her own rule and communicate with Starr. Heading toward her quarters, she opened her mind to him and was pleased to receive a response.

At the same time, she heard a soft knock at her cabin door and said, "Enter." Savvy came in and asked if she could join the conversation. Joy nodded and a three-way communication began.

Joy marveled that this was possible; when she was carrying Savvy, there was no one who was capable of participating in what was a mother-babe link. She would have to ask Savvy about it.

Chapter 9
Enter the Birds

Part of the cargo of both Ships were Sean's newly-designed birds. Once released into Space, a remote control on each Ship could direct them into the Black Hole. At a predetermined time, both Ships would meet at the near Black Hole and perform this function.

The primary message carried by the birds was one of invitation: an offer to establish diplomatic relations with the kingdoms of Akura. In addition, each bird carried a small capsule designed to bring a reply back to the Spaceport Base on Alteria.

This was the day that the birds would be sent on their mission. There was a heightened level of excitement on both Ships. At the appointed time, the birds were released and the two Captains used their remote controls to aim them into the mouth of the Black Hole.

The birds would send automatic reports from their onboard cameras as they flew into the Hole and beyond. These reports, including images, would be captured by recorders back on the Ships. Crew members on both Ships hovered around the recorders as images from the Black Hole were displayed on a vid screen in each Control Room.

The internal sides of the Hole seemed to be full of lightning bolts and swirling gases. Fortunately, Sean's new birds had a defense system and were not affected by what looked to be a dangerous passage.

As the birds proceeded, the gases increased in intensity and the lightning bolts were more frequent. It looked so dangerous. Finally, everything calmed down and light could be seen ahead.

When the birds exited the Black Hole, the landscapes ahead were much different than Akura's. Even though the two known kingdoms were very far apart, the two landscapes looked similar. The birds soared into the sky and the vid screens in both Ships amazed the crew members who were watching.

In the first landscape there were many residents walking about—in identical pairs! The two Captains were in constant communication as they observed the screens. Joy commented to Kert that, to her, each pair seemed to contain one human and one look-alike avatar. On rare occasions, when only one individual could be seen, Joy pointed that out—wondering why the presumed pair was incomplete.

Joy's birds flew in concentric circles, covering much of

the territory below. Kert's birds followed a similar pattern. The primary difference between the two sets of observations being transmitted by the birds was color: Joy's residents all wore bright colors; Kert's wore beige and black garments.

"I'm guessing that we're viewing two different kingdoms on this planet," suggested Joy.

Kert agreed, adding, "What do you think the colors indicate?"

"What color garments were the aliens captured by Sean wearing?" asked Joy.

"Black and beige," replied Kert. "I thought it was to make them inconspicuous, but now I believe it represented the kingdom that had sent them."

"That means they came through the Black Hole that is farthest away from Akura when it was still open," concluded Joy. "How long do you think we should just hang out here, Kert? My view is that we should return to Base and arrange for an Astral Journey through the closest Black Hole."

"I concur," said Kert. "We need more solid intel and that's the best strategy for getting it. We could do the Journey from our Ship, but that could be dangerous. If an invasion should come through either Black Hole while an Astral Journey is happening, our real bodies would be at significant risk."

The two Captains were in agreement and charted a course toward Akura. Joy sent a mental alert that they were coming home. The next step would be an Astral Journey.

*   *   *   *   *

When both Ships had safely landed back on Akura, the two Captains and Nolan hurried to Georgio's office to make their report. When they had finished, Georgio looked at them, asking, "Who would you recommend for this Astral Journey?"

Joy immediately volunteered, citing the numerous Time travels she had done. Kert admitted that he had no experience comparable to hers and, with personal difficulty, refrained from mentioning that she was with child.

Joy caught his eye and nodded gratefully, adding that it would be important for a Captain to remain on Base in case a hostile incursion came through one of the Holes and a defense needed to be suddenly mounted.

Nolan's name was added to the growing list. His background on an as yet unidentified planet and his flight through the Black Hole elsewhere in the universe were important arguments for his inclusion.

Savvy was listening outside the door and finally couldn't restrain herself. She burst into the office and practically demanded to be part of the Astral team. Her parents nodded their approval and Savvy smiled.

Georgio approved the recommended names, which also included several crew members of Explorer 3. The start of the mission was set for sun-up the next day and he recommended that everyone get a good night's sleep.

Chapter 10
The Astral Journey

The next morning, Joy met with the crew selected for this special assignment. She waved her arm and softly chanted. A flash of light and everyone was attired in clothes very similar to the apparel they had observed on the Ship's vid screen.

She explained that, while Astral Journeys are usually conducted with participants in an invisible state, occasionally it becomes necessary to let themselves be seen—and it would be important that they blended with the local population.

A room on Base had been outfitted with the requisite number of cots for their sleeping bodies. The cots were arranged so that everyone could hold hands during the Journey. Joy reminded them of the importance of maintaining physical contact; if anyone broke contact, the ability to return home could be compromised.

When everyone had reclined on a cot and taken the hand of another crew member, Joy ordered that their hands be bound together to reduce the danger of letting go. She then began to chant. A golden haze surrounded the group and, as they all fell asleep, their astral bodies rose into the air, through the ceiling and into the sky. The Astral Journey had begun.

Savvy was positioned between her parents as they led the Astral crew toward the nearby Black Hole. When Joy halted the group at the entrance to the Black Hole, Savvy could feel the pull—but it wasn't hard to resist, since their bodies had no mass.

Moving forward, they entered the Black Hole and let its pull propel them toward Planet A. Their rate of speed continued to grow and it was very soon that they began to view the light of the planet beyond the Hole's exit.

Flying out of the Hole toward Planet A, Joy and Nolan began to search for buildings that might be governmental in purpose. A large city appeared below them and, as they continued flying, they spied a likely building and descended to the surface.

As they walked toward the building, the newbies in the group were stunned when residents walked right through them. As Joy led them into the building through a side wall, that astonishment grew exponentially. By the time this mission was over, they would all feel like veterans.

Hearing voices, Joy led the group toward them and into a large conference room. They stopped in the rear of the room and stood against the wall. Savvy chanted softly and the voices were translated into a language understood by the Astral visitors. *"Just another Eighth Generation skill, Mama,"* whispered Savvy mentally.

The occupants of the room quieted down when another person entered. It became apparent that the newcomer was important and radiated power. As he spoke, Savvy temporarily labeled him Person 1. He related that their spies had successfully penetrated that part of the universe at the other end of the Black Hole. However, they were captured and, being avatars, were somehow made to self-destruct.

A question from the audience wanted to know if the change of clothing worked. Person 1 laughed and said that it was a complete success. "The naive residents of the planet we wish to invade already believe that it was our Adversary kingdom that was the author of the invasion. We received a detailed report from the avatars before they were vanquished."

"So it was our Adversary kingdom that conducted a defense through their Black Hole and was repelled by Ships from the other side?" asked another voice.

"That's correct," admitted Person 1. "We must revise our attack strategy before trying it again. By the way, we captured some robot birds that were carrying invitations to set up diplomatic relations with both our Adversary kingdom and ourselves. This is a perfect opportunity to make covert inroads without being seen as hostile!"

Everyone laughed and complimented Person 1 on a clever strategy. Person 1 smiled and added, "We will let them focus on our dull clothing pseudo threat while we 'make friends' and take over quietly. It's a perfect plan!"

Joy motioned to the group to follow her back through the wall. Using mental communication, she began, *"Well, this was a very useful mission so far. Without this Journey, we would have been dupes and totally unaware of this plot.*

"I want to find this other kingdom, the one they call their Adversary. Savvy, can you do that?"

"Yes, Mama," Savvy answered, *"I already calculated the coordinates. "I can take us there."*

As a group, they rose into the air and followed Savvy.

*   *   *   *   *

Flying over the planet to reach Savvy's coordinates, the group soon recognized the beige and black clothing of the residents below. *"This must be the 'Adversary' kingdom that we are seeking,"* pronounced Joy. *"Let's look for a city and government building at this location."*

Savvy soon pointed out a likely building and the group descended to the ground. As they walked toward it, they noticed that the residents were individuals, not look-alike pairs as in the previous kingdom.

Entering the building, they heard voices ahead. Joy led them toward the voices and, as they did in the other kingdom, they entered a large room through the wall and stood in the rear.

This was a smaller group than they had witnessed in the colorful kingdom. The setting was more informal and one speaker was seemingly in charge. Once again, Savvy cast a translation spell and they began to listen.

"Are you certain that we were not under attack?" asked Speaker #1.

"Yes sir," replied Speaker #2. "Our spies in the colorful kingdom are confident that we have been fed false intel."

"Do we know where those Spaceships that we fought originated?" another Speaker questioned.

"We do not," added Speaker #2. "But we have an idea. Some robotic birds were recovered coming toward us through another Black Hole. They carried friendly messages about diplomatic exchanges. It is possible that they are from whatever planet sent those Ships. When the Ship we are building is completed, we could retrace their cosmic signature to find that planet."

"Do our spies have any new intel about our Adversary

kingdom?" asked Speaker #1.

"Yes," replied Speaker #2, "and it is very disturbing. They have also received robotic birds and are planning to reply positively to the invitation—as a first step in a sneak attack on that friendly planet. We need to do something."

Chapter 11
Counter Measures

Joy sent a mental message to her team, *"This is why I created the clothing that we are wearing. I will now become visible to this gathering. You should remain cloaked unless a dangerous situation develops. Nolan will be in charge during this period."*

Chanting softly, Joy suddenly appeared in the midst of the Speakers. They looked stunned and reached for their weapons. However, Speaker #1 had a different approach.

"Welcome to our planet, Unknown Person," he said, extending his hand. "My name is Nikos and I am the Ruler of this kingdom, known as Thalia, on the planet Divos. I assume you heard me refer to an Adversary kingdom. Its name is Dubbell and half of its residents are avatars. The Ruler there changed the kingdom's name to reflect its new practice of every citizen having an avatar double. As you can see, we do not agree with having avatars."

"How many kingdoms are on your planet?" asked Joy.

"We have just the two established kingdoms," Nikos replied. "Elsewhere on the planet are pockets of people who are less developed in terms of organizational skills. That will happen eventually, but it will take time. Tell me, are you from the same planet as the robot birds?"

"Yes, I am," Joy confirmed. "I am here to answer any questions you may have. And I did hear your conversation before I showed myself. You are correct that you were not under attack. We believed that you were attacking us. Disinformation is such a terrible thing. Please accept my apology for the destruction of your Ships. We are a peaceful people."

Nikos nodded and invited Joy to sit next to him at the table. "Please tell us something about your planet and where it is located in the galaxy."

Joy was pleased to describe Akura and its peoples, but stopped short at providing a detailed description of its precise location. The twinkle in Nikos' eye let her know he was aware of what she was doing. At that moment, she received a mental message from Savvy saying that she and Starr had been analyzing Nikos and his friends, arriving at the conclusion that they were forthright and honest.

With that assurance in mind, Joy relaxed and became more outspoken about herself and her planet. Then she asked a blunt question, "What would you advise me about Dubbell and its intentions? I will need to design an effective defense strategy to thwart their underhanded scheme."

Her question sparked a lively discussion that produced some remarkable suggestions. She hoped her team was taking notes! When she heard an offer to support any preemptive strike through the Black Hole directly at Dubbell, she was astonished and was unable to speak for a moment.

She heard Nolan's voice in her mind cautioning her against making any actual commitments at this time. Nodding, she thanked Nikos and his companions, but let them know that she needed to bring this intel back to her planet before making any decisions. Savvy let her know that Nikos approved the wisdom of her statement. With that knowledge, she rose and took her leave, promising to be back in touch soon. Then she became invisible again.

But she didn't leave. She wanted to hear what they thought about her arrival and the conversation she and Nikos had just finished. She watched a cloaked Savvy inch closer to the table, casting a truth spell. There were no surprises in the discussion that ensued. These aliens had believed Joy and were actively trying to find ways to support her in any further encounters on their planet.

Joy then ended the Astral Journey and they awoke on the cots at the Base. She reminded the team that the results of their journey were to be considered top secret, as she and her family hurried off to Georgio's office to report.

*   *   *   *   *

The meeting with Georgio and Crystos was a lengthy affair. There was much intel to share and it soon became clear that Tamara, the Defense Team and the Council would need to become involved.

Georgio sent a mental message to Tamara with a summary of the Astral Journey's intel. She immediately called an emergency meeting to be held at Space Force Headquarters the next day. To be invited were not only the Astral Journey members, the Defense Team and the Council, but also the members of SC/United.

Tamara was convinced that any decisions would need to be approved by all affected parties. This was the first planet-wide crisis situation and Tamara was determined to have full participation.

*   *   *   *   *

When all invited parties had arrived at Space Force Headquarters the next day, Tamara could sense that emotions were high. This would not be an easy meeting of minds.

Chapter 12
The Meeting

Tamara called the meeting to order. When the clamor of voices had stilled, she asked Joy to summarize the conversation she had shared with Nikos the previous day.

Asking Nolan to help her remember all the details, Joy began to describe the Journey... and then moved on to the conversation itself. While she was speaking, Nolan monitored the reactions of the audience—which ranged from disbelief to outright panic.

Joy's description of what they had heard at the first kingdom they visited made Tamara's blood run cold. Clearly, not only her kingdom was being targeted—but the planet itself. She locked eyes with Sean, who was listening intently.

When Joy had finished her report, Tamara once again took over the meeting. She opened the session to questions—which were numerous and forthcoming. Although she tried to keep the meeting positive and productive, it was inevitable that an undercurrent of fear was present as well.

After the barrage of questions had ebbed, Tamara switched to a different approach. "Now that you understand what we are facing, I want you to start thinking creatively about how to defend our planet. We have all engaged in some kinds of altercations, whether with each other or, in Marinea's case, from another planet. But we have never encountered a threat of this magnitude, and one that promises to affect our well-being so deeply.

"Rather than try to brainstorm as a large group, I have a box with small colored glass balls that I will pass around. I want you to close your eyes, stir the balls and take a ball without looking at it. When you have done this, I will tell you how to proceed," she instructed.

When everyone had a ball, Tamara called in six staff members, each one with a colored sign: blue, red, yellow, white, orange and green. They stood along the walls, holding up their signs. Tamara told the audience that they should go to the color that matches the color of the ball they are holding.

After the audience had been separated by color, the staff members led their groups to separate rooms in the Headquarters complex to discuss ideas for defense.

Tamara sighed and hoped that mixing up the audience by color would lead to a better result than if they had organized themselves by friends or colleagues. The sub-group staff leaders would gather the intel at the end of the day and bring it to her for review. They would also tell their sub-groups to return to the main venue the next morning.

*   *   *   *   *

Tamara and Sean spent a long night analyzing and categorizing the accumulated intel. They were not surprised to find that one approach had overwhelming support: an offensive attack through the nearest Black Hole directly against the kingdom that threatened them. Emphasis had been placed on timing the attack as soon as possible, before that kingdom had begun to mount their planned offense.

"We have only two Ships to execute this recommendation," warned Sean. "Explorer 4 is close to completion, but is not yet ready. However, we have one distinct advantage; we know how to make the avatars self-destruct, which would eliminate at least half of the attack force."

"Actually, that estimate may be low," proposed Tamara. "This kingdom seems to use avatars as substitutes for humans. Perhaps it is only the avatars that we would be facing."

"You may be right," agreed Sean, "but we have to plan for the worst. I'm going to ask Sunan to return as soon as possible; we will need him."

"Be sure to let him know that I am reconvening our Kingdom delegates tomorrow morning and that I hope he can be here by then," reminded Tamara.

"I will, my Dear," Sean promised. "Try and get a nap before then. We have a busy day ahead." Giving her a loving kiss, he teleported to his office to make arrangements.

*   *   *   *   *

The next morning, Tamara welcomed the delegates back to continue defense planning. She reported that she and Sean had examined and organized the data from the sub-group meetings the day before. Letting them know that the overwhelming defense approach suggested by the data had been an immediate attack through the nearby Black Hole. That plan was being implemented as she spoke.

At that moment, Sunan entered the room and she re-introduced him to the delegates. A surge of applause responded to her comments and the delegates stood in support. One delegate moved that Queen Tamara and her Defense Team be authorized to conduct the defense on behalf of all the kingdoms on Akura. The motion passed with unanimous consent.

A second delegate asked if this meeting could be paused so that all delegates could return home and alert their governments. Tamara asked for their patience, as it was important that no intel leave this room until the attack had begun. Nodding, the delegates expressed their understanding, once again applauding as the Captains and crews of Explorers 1 and 3 hurried from the room.

Tamara had ordered a sumptuous breakfast for the delegates, which was now about to be served. Sunan bowed and told her he would be joining Sean as the defense of Akura began. Nodding, she wished him well and joined the delegates for breakfast.

Chapter 13
The Defense of Akura

Although Kert's status was senior to Joy's, he knew that she should lead the attack for two reasons: she was Sixth Generation and she had experience leading defense against intruders from the far Black Hole.

When it was time to begin their mission, with both Explorer Ships on their launching pads, he asked Joy to join him in his Ready Room. Presenting his argument with clarity and determination, he was a bit surprised that she offered no resistance.

"Are you certain, Kert?" she asked. "You do outrank me."

"Absolutely," he affirmed. "This mission requires us to use our resources to the best of our ability—and that requires you to take the lead. It also means that Sunan should be stationed on your Ship. He needs to be in the first wave in order to deactivate the avatars."

Nodding her agreement, Joy saluted and returned to her Ship to begin the countdown. A few minutes later, Sunan appeared in her Control Room. Kert must have contacted him.

"Where should I sit, Captain?" asked Sunan.

"Next to the Pilot, Your Majesty," Joy replied. "And grab a communications device. You may have to work your magic from a distance."

"Aye, Captain," smiled Sunan, "and please call me Sunan." He walked over to the Pilot and took a seat next to him. Feeling a touch on his arm, he looked up to find Savvy at his elbow. The last time he had seen her, she was a babe. Now she seemed to have grown into a very attractive young woman. What a mystery!

"Hello, Sunan," Savvy began. "I know we have met before, but I was quite a bit smaller. And yes, I have accelerated my growth in order to participate in adult responsibilities and activities. Right now, I am checking out the instruments here in the Control Room to get ready for lift-off."

Sunan looked at her with bewilderment. If what she was saying was true, this was a most marvelous development. Nolan had taken his place in the Second Chair and called over to Sunan, "She's telling you the truth. You'll get used to being amazed by her powers."

Sunan watched Savvy hurry over to her own chair and buckle herself in as Joy ordered, "Lift-off in 10…9…8…7…6…5…4…3…2…1!"

The rocket's engines roared and Explorer 3 headed into the atmosphere, soon reaching the stratosphere. In the Ground Control Room, technicians and scientists watched carefully; a second group began to focus on the countdown for Explorer 1. Soon both Ships had departed. The mission was underway.

*   *   *   *   *

The two Ships headed directly for the nearby Black Hole. As soon as it was safe to do so, Savvy stood and began to walk around the Control Room. She watched the many instruments carefully and mentally shared her findings with Starr and her parents.

As the transit continued, Starr sent Savvy an urgent message. "I can hear the sound of several incoming vessels heading toward us."

Savvy shared his intel mentally with her parents and Joy stood, ordering weapons at-the-ready. Sunan grabbed his communications device and began to chant the spell that would force the avatars to self-destruct. The Ship's Communication Officer turned and activated an external speaker so that the chant preceded them down the Black Hole.

Several spacecraft could be seen advancing toward them quickly…when a flash of light blinded the crew of Explorer 3. As their eyes began to focus again, no incoming vessels were visible.

Sunan clapped and crowed, "I always wondered if that spell could be used at a distance, without being part of the avatar internal network. Obviously, it could! That gives us a lot more latitude in our defense planning."

*   *   *   *   *

The two Explorer Ships continued into the Black Hole, all crew alert to encountering more hostile forces. Savvy chuckled to herself that the keenest ear aboard Exploreer 3 belonged to Starr! She could hardly wait until he was born so she could check what Generation he would be.

It wasn't long before a light could be seen ahead, indicating that the end of the Black Hole was near. Both Ships activated their new cloaking devices so that their presence could not be seen by the planet ahead. Once they were clear of the Hole and able to navigate around the planet Divos, it would be possible to send an Away Team on an Astral Journey.

Joy had decided on that strategy in order to protect Starr from any harm. She would be resting in her cabin while her astral self-led the astral search party.

As she made herself comfortable, she felt the Ship emerge from the Black Hole. A vid screen in her cabin allowed her to view the planet below. As she focused on the screen, she felt the first labor pain.

Crystal Saga Series 4

2 — Interplanetary Conflict

D. E. Weingand

Prologue

My name is Savvy. I am the first-born of Joy and Nolan. My mother is the first-born of Princess Candace of Marinea and Cecil, the Ruler of Freedom. Both kingdoms are on the planet Akura.

My father is an expatriate from an unknown planet on the other side of the universe…and an unidentified Super Child, which meant that he had no memories until he reached puberty. At that time, he recognized that the Resistance members who had taken charge of him did not share his values and he escaped through a far Black Hole by stealing a small Spacecraft.

My parents met at the Academy of Magic in Marinea and engaged in some Time travel escapades together. After graduating, they were advised by Terra, the Head Watcher, that they were 'true mates'…and the rest is history!

Super Children can be identified by using a certain spell that causes a number to appear on their foreheads. Most of my family are Generations 1 through 3—but I am a 8! Terra told us that Nolan would be upgraded to an 8 when we wed.

When I was born, after choosing to accelerate my development, I was identified as Generation 8! The abilities and powers at my disposal have already resulted in a victory within the far away Black Hole—when we made a mistake and thought the Spacecrafts coming toward us were hostile. Mama, during an Astral Journey, has apologized to the kingdom that sent them.

During that battle, our Ship (Explorer 2) was destroyed, leaving my father, a Captain, without a Ship. He has now been assigned to be Captain of Explorer 4, which is nearing completion. Until that time, he is serving as Second-in-Command to my mother, who is Captain of Explorer 3.

Explorers 1 and 3 are now on a mission to enter the near Black Hole and engage the hostile forces of Dubbell, one of the two major kingdoms on the planet Divos.

An important advantage is the presence of Sunan, the Ruler of the kingdom of Mesarra on the planet of Akura. He knows a spell which causes avatars to self-destruct—and half of the inhabitants of Dubbell are avatars. Sunan believes that the hostile vessels approaching us are staffed entirely by avatars.

As Sunan was saying the spell, our Communications Officer was broadcasting it outside and forward of our Ship. There was a bright light and when we could see again, no vessels were visible. We assume that the avatars' self-destruction was responsible.

Before we engaged the enemy, I was walking around the Control Room checking on our instruments. At first, the crew was disturbed by my presence, as I was much smaller when I boarded. However, now I look like a young woman and they have come to terms with having me around. I had accelerated my development again in order to make this happen.

As I monitored the instruments, I came close to where my mother was seated in the Command Chair. I heard something and stopped my inspection. Following the sound, I discovered that it came from my mother's tummy! Listening carefully, I learned that my mother was carrying a new babe inside—a male and my brother!

After sharing this news with my parents, I continued to have communication with my brother—who preferred the name Starr. Before I was born, my mother and I could easily communicate, which was a 'first' at the time. My ability to be a third voice in the conversation between my mother and Starr is another 'first'.

Mother is scheduled to lead the Astral Journey that will take place once we exit the Black Hole near Divos. She has asked Starr to talk to ME until we return to Base as she has a lot on her plate until then. He did seem to agree and our conversations have continued.

I noticed that Mother had retired to her cabin for a rest until we reached Divos. Then I heard her cry out!

Chapter 1
Arrival at Divos

The cloaked Explorers 3 and 1 exited the Black Hole and began to orbit the planet Divos. A large cabin on Explorer 3 had been designated as the location where the bodies of the Astral Journey Away Team would sleep during the mission.

Captain Joy would lead the Astral Journey, accompanied by Sunan and three crew members. Nolan would take over Command while Joy was on the Journey. But now there was a complication. Joy's cry had alerted Nolan and Savvy, who hurried to her side.

They found that Dr. Jeen had already arrived. The doctor looked at Nolan and shook her head, "Captain Joy is unable to lead the Astral Journey," she informed him. "Her babe is demanding to be born."

Joy complained, "He wouldn't wait!"

Savvy told her, "Mama, I tried. But he has a stubborn streak."

"We need to conduct that Astral Journey in order to find out what we're up against," Joy ordered as she began to pant. "Nolan, you are in command of the Ship. Savvy, you are the only one who has the necessary experience to lead the Astral Journey. Are you up for the challenge?"

"Yes, Mama," affirmed Savvy. "I can do it. Don't worry. And Starr says he will make his birth a quick one—and he'll take care of you."

"Who is Starr?" asked the doctor.

"My brother," answered Savvy, "who is about to be born. Mama, I need to organize the Away Team now." She kissed Joy on the forehead and left the cabin. Nolan watched her go with both pride and amazement on his face.

*   *   *   *   *

Savvy rounded up Sunan and the three designated crew members, who had also participated in the first Astral Journey, and led them into the cabin arranged for their use. She explained that she would be substituting for the Captain, who was unable to lead the Away Team. The three crew members accepted the change without protest, but Sunan seemed to be hesitant.

"*Do you have questions, Sunan?*" asked Savvy mentally.

"*I do, yes*," admitted Sunan, responding mentally to her query. "*I saw you recently and you were so much smaller. You told me you accelerated your development. Are you sure you are capable to leading this very important Astral Journey?*"

"*Absolutely,*" Savvy asserted. "*My mother, the Captain, is a Generation 6. I am a Generation 8 and some very important skills come with that designation. Do you trust me?*"

Sunan nodded and saluted. "Proceed, Savvy."

The Away Team took their places on the cots as Savvy chanted a spell and their hands were bound to each other. She continued chanting and their bodies fell asleep as their Astral selves rose into the air. They left the Ship through a side panel and headed down to the kingdom of Dubbell.

Since Savvy had been part of the first Astral Journey to this planet, she knew exactly where to lead the team. They entered through the wall of the same room where the first team had encountered the Ruler of Dubbell and his cohorts.

It was as if no time had passed. The same plotters were in the room and the Ruler was shouting at them. "Can anyone tell me what happened to our vessels and their crews? They just disappeared."

Those in the room looked at each other helplessly; they had no idea. The Ruler was becoming increasingly upset.

"We have to find out! How can we mount an offense if we don't know what we're up against?" he cried. "I'm sending all of you and your Shadows to the construction sites to gather intel. You have permission to use whatever 'persuasion' you need to get some answers! We will reconvene tomorrow morning."

In a few minutes, the room was empty.

Sunan sent a mental message to Savvy, *"It looks to me as if they are totally unaware of what caused the destruction of their vessels and crews. But what are 'Shadows'?"*

"I believe they are referring to their avatars," replied Savvy. *"Sunan, your ability to cause their self-destruction is definitely our secret weapon.*

"Let's move on to the other kingdom now," she ordered, leading the Away Team through the wall and into the air. The two kingdoms were not close together, but the transit didn't take long at all.

*   *   *   *   *

"This kingdom is named Thalia," Savvy informed the Away Team, as they landed near the building visited by the first Astral Journey. As before, she knew where she was going and headed straight for it.

Inside the building, Savvy moved through the wall of the room she had visited before. But no one was inside. Returning to the hallway, she heard some voices from above a stairway. Leading the Team up the stairway, she found the Ruler, Nikos, chatting with one of his aides. Mentally asking her Team to stay invisible, she waved her hand and was clad in clothes commonly worn in this kingdom. Making herself visible, she walked toward Nikos.

Nikos looked surprised, but then warmly welcomed her return. "Is your mother with you?" he asked.

"Not this time," she responded. "She is welcoming my brother into this world."

"Really!" Nikos exclaimed. "Please give her my best wishes. How can I help you today?"

"I've come to get the latest intel from you about Dubbell and its intentions. What can you share with me?" asked Savvy.

"My undercover spies in that kingdom tell me that the Ruler has sent his spies into the streets to question residents, using whatever means are necessary." he reported. "He is acting like a crazy person because he can't figure out what happened to the vessels and crews in his last incursion into the Black Hole near his kingdom. Be careful…he is very dangerous, especially when he feels threatened."

Savvy thanked Nikos for the intel and asked if he had any advice for how her planet should proceed in designing its defense. Nikos sighed with frustration but reminded her that they would support whatever decisions would be made. Savvy nodded and vanished, leaving Nikos shaking his head.

Chapter 2
Meanwhile, on Explorer 3

Dr. Jeen wiped Joy's forehead and urged her to breathe deeply. Nolan was holding Joy's hand as she cried, "I need to push!"

When she did so, a tiny babe emerged and the doctor looked stunned. "This isn't possible!" she exclaimed. "Your babe should be much larger."

Joy leaned back on her pillow and laughed, "Don't worry, Doctor. He will be very soon."

As they watched, the babe shivered and grew...and grew...and grew! Soon he was the size of a normal newborn and looked around the cabin. He held his arms out to Joy and patted her cheek, sending her a mental message of love and support. She smiled and told everyone, "His name is Starr."

Nolan looked stunned at the whole experience. He knew he should be ready to accept whatever happened, but this was beyond his expectations. He watched the doctor clean the newborn, accepting the swaddled babe as Starr reached for him. Looking down at his son, Nolan received the first message from him, "*Hello, Da,*" Starr offered, "*It's nice to finally meet you. Please don't be shocked when I continue to increase the pace of my growth. I promised Savvy that I would take care of Mama."*

As Nolan held Starr, he was startled to see him visibly increasing in size. The doctor fainted.

*   *   *   *   *

Later that day, a bed appeared next to Joy's and Starr teleported into it. He was now the size of a small child and looked sleepily at the bed. *"Mama,"* he said, *"I am quite tired after growing so fast. I need to take a sleep now. You will be safe, I promise,"* he sighed and fell fast asleep.

Joy held Nolan's hand and sighed. "Mama told me that my insistence on growing faster was a challenge. I never understood why she would say that—but I do now! And Starr is affecting his development a lot more and faster than I could."

Nolan kissed her cheek and commented, "We knew we were in for a unique parental experience, Dear. I believe that the Away Team is about to finish its Astral Journey. I'm going to the cabin where their bodies are sleeping and wait for Savvy. We need to know what number Starr's Generation is—and Savvy is the only one who can tell us. She has memorized the spell."

Leaving Joy to take a much-needed rest, Nolan left her cabin.

*   *   *   *   *

When he reached the cabin containing the cots occupied by the Away Team, they were just regaining consciousness. Nolan walked over to Savvy's cot and asked her to follow him.

When she asked about her mother, he explained everything that had transpired. "Starr was so tiny when he was born, he looked like a small doll. But that soon changed," he said. "Your mother and I would like you to cast the spell that identifies his Generational status."

Savvy nodded and they hurried to Joy's cabin. Trying not to awaken Joy, Savvy chanted softly and she watched her brother's forehead closely. Nolan gasped when the number appeared: it was 10!

*   *   *   *   *

"It's more than mine!" exclaimed Savvy. "How is that possible?"

"I have a theory," murmured Nolan. "On the Astral Journey that your mother led, they passed through the Black Hole—which has a lot of magnetic energy. Perhaps it influenced his initial development."

"But their bodies were here," Savvy mentioned.

"I realize that," Nolan continued. "But we don't know everything about how Astral Journeys affect the actual body, especially when it is just forming."

"Wait a minute!" Savvy pondered. "Mama's body didn't go through the Black Hole—but yours did! When you escaped and came to Akura! What if it was YOUR body that changed? It made no sense to me at the time that I should be Eighth Generation when Mama was Sixth.

"And now my brother, who should be like me, is another leap forward! Da, I think YOU are the missing piece of this puzzle," she concluded.

"So, are you suggesting that every member of the crews on our two Ships, if they become parents, will have similar results? That would cause chaos!" Nolan predicted.

A flash of light and Terra had joined them. "The Creator Being and I have been watching you closely. You have correctly identified the causality of how Black Holes affect the human genome," she asserted.

"Until a way is discovered to insulate the Ships from the effects of the Black Holes, I have brought a potion that should be replicated and distributed to all crew members on all Ships entering the Black Holes," she stressed. "Savvy, your Eighth Generation abilities will enable you to oversee this project."

Handing the potion to Savvy, Terra vanished.

Dr. Jeen had entered the cabin to check on Joy and had

overheard Terra's explanation. She sighed and walked over to Savvy and Nolan.

"Please come with me to my lab and we will work with that potion immediately. I'm guessing that it might be time-sensitive," she suggested. "When we have created a sufficient quantity, you can teleport some over to Explorer 1."

Savvy nodded and left the cabin with the doctor.

Chapter 3
The Mission Continues

Nolan sat at Joy's bedside, watching her begin to wake up. She smiled at him and reached out to hold his hand. "What has happened while I've been sleeping?" she asked.

"Our known understanding of the universe has changed," Nolan began, and he proceeded to bring her up-to-date on the Astral Journey and the new intel about effects of Black Holes.

"So Savvy and the doctor are working to replicate Terra's potion?" Joy inquired.

"Yes," confirmed Nolan. "And when they are finished, I'm going to ask Dr. Jeen to do a complete work-up on me to see what other mutations might be occurring in my body."

Joy threw her blankets aside and started to stand; Nolan hastened to assist her. "Don't worry, Dear. I'm fine. My Sixth Generation self is quite capable of assuming full duties. I need to contact Captain Kert to alert him that neither Ship should enter the Black Holes until everyone aboard has ingested the potion."

She walked over to Starr's bed to check on him. He smiled in his sleep—then suddenly opened his eyes. A huge shiver enveloped his body as another growth spurt occurred.

Joy sighed, wishing that he had stayed a babe a little longer. Because fatigue had put her to sleep, she hadn't been able to hold him…and now, he was too big to do so. His growth had progressed so much that he looked ready to enter school!

As she sat on his bed, he crawled out of his covers and onto her lap. "Mama," he said, "I know you want to hold me. I'd like to hold you, too."

"You can speak!" Joy stammered. "How wonderful! Were you listening to your father's briefing on what's been happening?"

"Of course," Starr replied. "I can absorb conversation even when I'm asleep. I hear Savvy and the doctor approaching. Be sure to take your dose right away."

"I will," promised Joy. "How much more growth are you going to produce? Living as a child can be fun."

"I understand that," Starr acknowledged, "but I've made certain promises to Savvy that I intend to honor, Mama. I intend to keep growing until I have reached adulthood."

"Oh my," protested Joy. "Is that really necessary?"

"Yes, Mama," he answered. "There are some dark days coming and we must be ready."

"How do you know that?" asked Nolan.

"My Generation Ten status allows mental Time travel, Da," he revealed. "That may be why the Creator Being allowed the jump to such a high level." Giggling, he added, "I don't suppose Savvy liked finding that out?"

Nolan admitted, "She was a bit perturbed."

Just then, as Starr had predicted, Savvy and the doctor entered the room. Dr. Jeen carried a large tray containing doses of the potion. Joy and Nolan both grabbed a dose. Starr declined, claiming he didn't need it. Savvy mentioned that she and the doctor had already taken theirs. When the doctor looked at Starr's current size, she shook her head as she left the room to distribute the doses to the crew.

"Starr," Savvy inquired, "why didn't you take a dose of the potion?"

"I don't need it," Starr replied. "I'm immune to the Black Hole effects."

"You're what??" cried Savvy. "Because the Holes caused your status jump?"

"That's right," agreed Starr. "And that will be very useful one day."

Savvy sank into a nearby chair. Her head was beginning to hurt! She needed to get her brother alone so they could get on the same page with their abilities!

*　　*　　*　　*　　*

Once both Ships' crews had received doses of the potion, the two Captains and their Executive Officers met in Joy's Ready Room. Also present was Savvy, since she had led the Astral Journey, and Sunan, who would be in charge of the self-destruct effort. It was time to create a battle plan.

Savvy proposed that they create colorful clothing for those crew members who would land on the planet which would match what the inhabitants wore. She also suggested that they ask Starr to place a glamour on each set of members of the landing party so that they looked alike. Fitting in would be a major asset for remaining incognito.

Sunan nodded his approval, then advised capturing several avatars so that he could insert his spell into their neural network. That would be the most efficient method for covering the entire kingdom.

A knock at the door revealed Starr standing in the doorway. He walked over to Savvy and conjured up another chair. He levitated himself into it and whispered in Savvy's ear. "Starr would like to be included in this planning," she said. "He has the ability of mentally assessing the future for each strategy that we consider. That would be a significant advantage. May he stay?"

Chapter 4
Another Secret Weapon

Sunan clapped and chuckled, "We need every weapon we can get! I vote to let him stay. This will be a more interesting meeting. What's that quote? 'From the mouths of babes?'"

Starr's face turned red and Savvy defended him, "Don't ridicule him, Sunan. He's a Gen 10 with much to offer!"

"A 10?" Sunan sputtered. "Are you sure? That's amazing!"

Joy interrupted, "We can discuss Starr's status some other time. But before we get back to planning our defense, I need to remind all of you to take the potion that is being passed around. It is essential that you do so in order to survive the Black Hole transit."

Everyone in the room nodded soberly. They understood the seriousness of her warning. When order was restored, she summarized the results of the glass ball exercise that Tamara had administered at the previous day's meeting.

"There was a strong consensus for taking an offensive initiative by sending our two Spaceships through the Black Hole to the kingdom of Dubbell. I'd like to use that consensus as a starting point for our discussion today," she proposed.

*   *   *   *   *

Hours later, a defense strategy had been outlined that would begin with a transit of the near Black Hole. Once successfully orbiting the planet of Divos in a cloaked state, an Away Team would be tasked with identifying and securing a small number of avatars and teleporting them back to Explorer 3.

After confining them in a secure cabin, Sunan would be charged with inserting his spell into their neural network—and, by doing so, into the bodies of every avatar on the planet. The planning paused there.

Joy looked at Starr and asked him for an analysis of whether that would be sufficient to be successful as a complete defense. Starr replied that as far as the planning had gone, it would be effective. He was unclear beyond that point, since they had no intel pointing to any other approaches.

"I think we need to be open to emerging ideas as we proceed. I will continue to monitor the situation," he promised.

Ending the planning session, Joy advised everyone to get a good night's sleep. The invasion would begin at 0800 tomorrow.

*   *   *   *   *

That evening, Joy had dinner with her family, plus Sunan,

18

in her quarters. By this time, Starr had reached adult size and he told them that his control over his physical development had ended. Joy admired the appearance of her fully grown son, but felt cheated that she had been deprived of being personally involved in the process. She did not feel a mother-son bond; he was a stranger.

Starr was quiet during the meal, which was an unusual state for him. Joy wondered if something was bothering him. She sent him a mental message asking if she could help. His response was worrisome. He admitted that he was uneasy, even though the defense planning had seemed to be on target. He sensed that something was missing.

"Missing?" she inquired. *"What do you mean?"*

"It feels like there is a gap in our planning...a 'missing piece'," he tried to explain. *"But I can't identify it."*

His comments were disconcerting to Joy and she began to worry. *"Do you think it's some strength possessed by the residents of Dubbell that we haven't noticed?"* she asked.

"Possibly," Starr answered. *"Or a weakness in our planning that we've overlooked."*

Joy decided to bring this conversation to the attention of the rest of those at dinner. Once she had briefed them, she opened it up for their thoughts and questions.

Sunan pondered the problem and offered, "If the 'missing piece' is part of either offense or defense, we need to figure it out before proceeding. My knowledge of avatars suggests that there might be something related to their internal communications system. Perhaps it works differently than the one we were able to infiltrate. I know it worked once for us with this group, but could they have countered with a way to defend against it?"

"Or might they have another group of avatars that operate differently?" mused Nolan.

"There are two strategies that we could try," suggested Savvy. "I can lead another Astral Journey to Thalia to see what they know...and Mama can travel the arc of Time to check on some potential outcomes of our present planning."

"I already did a future search," protested Starr. "I didn't detect any problems."

"What exactly did you see?" pressed Savvy.

"Once we orbited the planet, Sunan chanted his spell and the avatars self-destructed," Starr reported.

"And what happened?" demanded Savvy. "Did they turn into ash?"

"No," he admitted. "They just fell down."

"That's the problem!" cried Sunan. "They were damaged, but

not destroyed!!! I need to re-design the spell and test it on captive avatars."

"We have been meeting with Sean and he has informed us that there have been more incidents of sabotage around our planet," Georgio reported.

"When we originally had some spies in custody, Sunan did effectively cause them to self-destruct. But I agree with Sunan that there apparently has been a change in those avatars who visited the spies. Those visitors were damaged by Sunan's method, but were not destroyed," concluded Georgio.

Standing, Sunan cried, "I'll get to work right away!" He rushed to the door and left Joy's cabin.

*　　*　　*　　*　　*

After Sunan had left, the conversation resumed. Georgio continued, "In addition, when we plot out where there have been instances of sabotage around our planet, it is clear that there must still be many avatar spies who are actively working against us—and learning our weaknesses as they do so."

"That is terrifying!" responded Joy. "How can we help?"

"Our first priority is for Sunan to revise his method. . .and then figure out how to identify the at-large avatars," replied Georgio.

Joy was dismayed. She would have to postpone tomorrow's invasion until Sunan had been able to create a working spell. She hoped the delay would not prove to be a critical one.

Chapter 5
The New Spell

The next morning, after experiencing a restless night's sleep, Joy went looking for Sunan. She found him in the Ship's lab. The dark circles under his eyes told her that he had worked through the night.

"Any success?" she asked.

"I've created several new spells," he began, "but without any avatars to test them on, I can't be sure any of them will succeed."

"I'm going to ask Nolan to take Command while I visit the arc of Time," Joy proposed. "I'd like to take you with me. You should be able to determine what works, if any, by doing so. Meet me in my cabin."

*　　*　　*　　*　　*

When Sunan knocked at her cabin door, she invited him in and showed him to a room with cots inside. "This is my 'Travel Room,'" she explained. "We will journey to the arc of Time via the Astral plane. It is essential that we bind our hands together in order to maintain contact throughout the experience. Our mental link will be active throughout."

Joy put a 'Do Not Disturb" notice on her door and joined Sunan in the Travel Room. After they joined hands, she activated the Astral component of their Journey. Their Astral selves floated up to and through the ceiling of the room, exiting the Ship and landing on the arc of Time.

Slowly moving forward in Time, they observed Sunan trying different spells on avatars down on the planet. None of the spells seemed to work, which was disheartening. Joy noticed a human coming toward the group of avatars.

"Have you completed the defense component in your neural system?" asked the human.

"Yes, Sir," replied the avatar. "It is hard-wired and cannot be breached."

"*So that's what they've done,*" Sunan commented mentally to Joy. "*If I can gain access to just one avatar, I can overcome that component.*"

"*What do you need to make that happen?*" asked Joy.

"*My physical body in proximity to the body of an avatar. I would spell it into a sleep state and do a quick dismantling of his neural system. At that point, I can insert my command while the avatar is vulnerable. The fact that it is hard-wired is actually a benefit for us,*" added Sunan.

"*The meeting we are watching is actually taking place tomorrow. We will need to insert ourselves into the Timeline today,*"

24

Joy informed him. *"I will bring us back from the arc immediately. Make sure you remember everything about this location so we can teleport to it."*

Sunan nodded and Joy returned them to her cabin. Sitting next to him on his cot, she instructed him to teleport both of them to that memorized location. She made sure they were cloaked and could not be seen.

When they arrived, they were pleased to see that only one avatar was present. Grabbing the avatar's arms, they teleported back to Joy's cabin. Sunan spelled the avatar until it lost consciousness and proceeded to make the necessary alterations to its neural system.

Joy called some crew members to move the unconscious avatar to a holding cell. She then contacted Explorer 1, initiating a call for immediate entry into the near Black Hole.

Explorer 3 was first into the Hole. She was surprised to see that Explorer 1 was just behind. Starr winked at her and crowed that he could 'move mountains!' She smiled and the two Ships proceeded toward Divos and the kingdom of Dubbell.

As they entered orbit above Dubbell, she teleported the sleeping avatar down to the surface in the center of the city. Sunan activated the altered neural system of the avatar and it self-destructed.

Other signs of avatar self-destruction were observed all over the planet.

Sunan then teleported an Away Team down to the Avatar Lab so that they could destroy all vestiges of avatar development. Joy led a second Away Team to the office of the Ruler of Dubbell.

When her Team became visible in his office, he backed away in fear. "You have sent spies to my planet. That is an act of war," she declared. "We have eliminated all avatars on your planet. Your hostile actions cannot continue. You and your followers will be detained until representatives from the other major kingdom on this planet can join us for discussions about peace."

*   *   *   *   *

The two Ships remained in orbit as they waited for the representatives from Thalia to arrive. Peace negotiations are never easy, but the Captains of the two Ships were confident that progress could be made. Mediators from Akura were brought to Divos on the newly-commissioned Explorer 4. Since Nolan was the designated Captain of that Ship, he assumed Command immediately. New Executive Officers would need to be appointed for both Explorer 3 and Explorer 4.

*   *   *   *   *

Explorer 1 was ordered to remain in orbit over Divos until the peace talks had concluded—satisfactorily. While diplomatic exchanges were ongoing, no conclusions had yet been reached.

The other two Ships were recalled to Base for crew changes. Joy was looking forward to conducting training exercises with a new crew. Her experienced crew would be awarded two months of liberty in recognition of their service during the Black Hole initiative.

Nolan had an inexperienced skeleton crew on Explorer 4, who had been assigned because of the need to transport the mediators to Divos. More crew members needed to be recruited, plus a new Executive Officer, before a training mission could be undertaken.

Change was in the air.

Chapter 6
Space Force 2.0

The Space Force had survived its growing pains. It had been a tumultuous experience for everyone—and fraught with danger. Hopefully, the diplomatic efforts on Divos would soon bear fruit. The crew on Explorer 1 looked forward to more interesting duty. Life aboard ship was often boring as the talks continued on the planet's surface.

Captain Kert continually reminded his officers that the crew had performed with distinction in a totally unknown situation. No one had ever experienced the transit through a Black Hole before. Their mission would go down in history.

However, he recognized that the crew deserved—and needed—some time off. He hoped that replacements would arrive soon. He had heard rumors that Explorer 5 was nearing completion. Perhaps relief was coming.

*　　*　　*　　*　　*

While their Ships were being made ready for new adventures, Joy and Nolan prepared a rare family dinner at home. Both Savvy and Starr would be there and everyone was looking forward to being together.

Conversation centered around their time aboard Explorer 3 and the challenges they faced. Sunan's name was brought up several times and how important he was to a positive outcome with the avatars. He was now back in Mesarra with Merlynn, enjoying some down time.

As they were enjoying their dinner, the personal communicators of both Captains went off. Sighing, they read the messages and told their children that their leaves had been cancelled and they were recalled to Base.

"But what about us?" asked Savvy and Starr at the same time.

"You can come with us to Base while we see what's going on," answered Nolan. "Then we will discuss it."

Hastily putting some clothes in bags, they teleported to Base. Georgio and Crystos were in their offices. Knocking first at Georgio's door, they entered when invited.

"Commander," Joy began, "we received a message on our communicators that our leaves were cancelled. What's going on?"

"I'm sorry that had to happen," apologized Georgio, "but we have a situation."

"What kind of situation?" pressed Nolan.

"While Sunan has successfully changed his method, cleansing Divos and Akura of avatars, we continue to hear reports of sabotage on our own planet," Georgio admitted. "Since this is still happening, even after Sunan's change of spell, we are convinced that the present spies on Akura are NOT avatars, but the human counterparts of the avatars who were eliminated."

"So what now?" asked Joy. "How do we locate and identify these human spies?"

"I don't know," admitted Georgio. "I've asked Crystos to join us in a brainstorming session...ah, I hear him at the door now."

Entering, Crystos pulled up a chair. "I understand we have a new problem," he said.

Starr stood and began pacing the room. "I can identify avatars," he stressed, "but humans are not distinct in any way. What kinds of sabotage are taking place?"

"Various kinds," sighed Georgio. "It's almost as if they are experimenting with what works best. Some are explosive; others are basic, like throwing rocks through windows. Then there have been poisonings of water supplies and derailment of trains. In rural areas, there have been traffic disruptions; in volcanic regions, lava has been diverted. It's more than nuisance...it's fomenting deliberate chaos."

Starr thought a moment. "It seems like various forms of distraction to me. Savvy, what do you think?"

"Are there any commonalities, Sir?" asked Savvy. "Does anything happen just before a chaotic event?"

"I can answer that," interrupted Crystos. "Just before something negative occurs, there seems to be a disruption in radio waves. That might be caused by some sort of weapon or communication device. I'm not sure."

"That's actually very helpful," stressed Starr. "Right now a disruption like you are describing is taking place by Explorer 5." And he vanished.

When he returned, he had several persons in custody, secured together. He had relieved them of some unfamiliar-looking weapons and deposited them on Georgio's desk. "These suspects were about to do something to Explorer 5," he reported.

Georgio sent for Security to remove the suspects to a holding cell. "How did you know?" he asked Starr.

"It's one of my abilities, Sir," Starr replied. "I can detect unusual sounds and disruptions in the ether—and find them instantly."

"What is your range, Son?" asked Crystos.

"Untested, Sir," admitted Starr. "But perhaps these detainees will provide some clues to further disruptions. May I be present during their interrogation?"

"Of course," Georgio agreed. "In fact, I'd like to invite all of you to accompany me to the holding cell. Please cloak yourselves first."

Chapter 7
The Holding Cell

When they reached the holding cell, Savvy poked her brother and asked, *"Do you see anything odd about those prisoners?"*

Starr looked carefully and poked her back, *"Well done, Sis. You see that faint glow, don't you?"*

"I do," she replied. *"What do you think causes it?"*

"I don't THINK...I KNOW!" Starr cried mentally. *"They're RADIOACTIVE!"* Even though he was cloaked, he cast a white haze into the cell, covering himself and all the other Space Force members as well. Then he started to chant silently and coated everyone other than the prisoners in a pink haze that sparkled and eventually dissipated.

"What did you do?" asked Savvy.

"I cleansed everyone other than the prisoners," Starr explained. *"You are all safe now."*

"Why not the prisoners?" Savvy inquired.

"It's evidence," he explained. *"We need to find out what is going on and why they are radioactive."* Then he let Georgio into their conversation and also summoned Sean to join them.

35

When he had fully briefed the two Commanders, he advised them to focus on the locations of all instances of sabotage. Then he shared his spell with them so they could decontaminate those sites.

Sean was shaking his head. *"Are you telling us that the multiple cases of sabotage were actually distractions so that the radiation could be implanted without being noticed?"*

"I believe so, Sir," confirmed Starr. *"It was truly a sneak attack."*

Sean had fortunately brought his memory-wiper with him and proceeded to erase the past few minutes from everyone's minds. When he was asked why the prisoners were coated with a white haze, he offered a reasonable response that it was to calm and control them. Only those who had 'need-to-know' clearance retained their full memories.

Sean had arrived with a small cadre of Security Force members and he instructed them to escort everyone not authorized from the holding cell area. He asked Starr and Savvy to remain for a minute.

"Do you have any suspicions or theories that you wish to share with me?" he asked them. "The two of you have higher Generation status than anyone else."

"Actually, I do, Sir," admitted Starr. "And I want to compliment

Savvy on recognizing that the detainees had a soft glow about them.

"I previously said that I'm able to identify avatars, but not humans," he continued. "But now I think I can. I believe that soft glow is traceable. If I cast a planet-wide spell, I think your birds could be adapted to target the location of radioactive spies. It's worth a try."

"I agree," Sean decided. "I'll make the adaptations to some of my birds right away. Stop by my office tomorrow and we'll send them on their way."

Starr and Savvy promised but remained at the holding cell to observe Sean's interrogation.

*   *   *   *   *

The next morning, the two siblings knocked at Sean's office door. "Did you learn anything from your questioning after we left?" asked Savvy.

"Very little," admitted Sean. "They did express sadness that their personal avatars had been eliminated—but they refused to divulge any clues as to their purpose on our planet…or the number of spies that are currently operating here."

"So it's time for us to go on the offensive," stressed Starr. "Are your birds ready to fly?"

"They are," said Sean. "Let's teleport them to the Space Force Base."

On the Base, Sean released his birds as Starr chanted a new spell that would surround the entire planet of Akura. Monitoring their progress on a tablet, Sean was more than a little surprised to see a large number of markers appear planet-wide.

"Papa," exclaimed Savvy, "that's a huge number of indicators. Surely that many spies can't be operating here."

"It's upsetting," Sean agreed, "but the data doesn't lie. However, I was prepared for such an outcome. I inserted a weapon in each bird's beak that would send a disabling ray to incapacitate each spy—and sending a locator message back to me."

"That's brilliant!" crowed Savvy. "Will you bring the culprits to the Security Force detention center?"

"Yes," Sean responded. "That's the next step. After that, I haven't decided our path forward."

"May I suggest creating a penal colony on an uninhabited planet?" Starr proposed. "Or...I understand that Marinea located a suitable planet for the inhabitants of Planet X when it was threatened by a supernova. Perhaps they would welcome some memory-wiped immigrants?"

"Those are two possibilities…and there may be others," Sean said. "I'll take it under advisement. Step 1 is to locate and incarcerate the offenders. That process starts right now."

*   *   *   *   *

While Sean was occupied with overseeing this major endeavor, the peace talks were continuing on Divos. The Ruler of Dubbell was being held under house arrest and was not allowed to participate in the talks. Once a decision was reached about the future of the soon-to-be incarcerated spies, he would be added to that group.

On Divos, an underlying situation was emerging from the kingdom of Thalia. The Resistance movement was still active. The violent actions and planning of that group kept surfacing during the talks. The two kingdoms seemed very far apart as the issues were discussed.

The mediators who had been imported from Akura had their hands full. Progress was slow and painful; tempers on both sides kept flaring and interrupting the efforts of the mediators. Hope and good intentions were in short supply. The main bone of contention seemed to be a large territory that lay between the two warring kingdoms. That territory was reputed to contain natural resources which were desired by both kingdoms.

Chapter 8
The Negotiations

Once the mediators became aware of the desirability of that territory, their path forward became much clearer. Surely a planet of that size would have other similar resource-rich areas. Could Sean's birds be borrowed to do a scan of the entire planet that would identify where such resources were located?

Sean was contacted by the mediation team. Before agreeing to their request, he felt compelled to consult Tamara for advice. She had more experience dealing with other planets than he—and no one possessed more diplomatic skills. Her handling of Planet X had impressed the kingdoms on Akura. Perhaps she had some insights into the problems Divos was experiencing.

Stopping by her office, Sean invited her to take a break and join him in the garden. Her eyes gleamed and she happily agreed. Walking hand-in-hand, they found an empty bench and claimed it.

Tamara had a sense that Sean's invitation was more complicated than needing a break. As they sat together, she began to ask Sean some gentle questions—seeking an entry into his true purpose. Finally, he turned to her and laid out the parameters of what the mediators were asking.

"That seems to be a reasonable request," Tamara commented. "But you are not sure that is the appropriate path forward?"

"I'm concerned that it would seem like interference from another planet," he admitted. "The development of Divos is much different than what we have experienced here on Akura. There are only two kingdoms of similar size—and they cannot get along. The rest of the planet is barely developed politically. My guess is that it will be some time before they can participate in diplomatic interactions."

"Do you feel that we are in danger of being drawn into conflict with Divos?" Tamara asked.

"I fear that could be a possibility," Sean responded.

"Then it is a matter of our national security," Tamara concluded. "We need more intel. Please inform the mediators that we will grant their request, but the operation will be handled by Marinea. We will share pertinent intel with them after we analyze what the birds discover."

Sean felt like a huge load had been lifted from his shoulders and he thanked Tamara, kissing her deeply. He stood and saluted, teleporting back to his office.

*   *   *   *   *

The next day, a squadron of birds was deployed through the near Black Hole, its mission to scan Divos for both resources and populated areas. Results were transmitted back to Sean's office in real time. A group of Security Force analysts worked with the data as it arrived. By the end of the day, a report was on Sean's desk and he took it to Tamara.

Sean and Tamara spent the evening going over the report. One thing stood out in the data: the two major kingdoms had been taking advantage of the emerging pockets of population growth. Both kingdoms had encouraged immigration, draining the best and brightest. Neither kingdom had fostered communication with the smaller population areas or treated them with respect. It was not surprising that the two large kingdoms would ultimately turn to conflict with each other in their urge to dominate the planet.

"I guess we can be grateful that our history on Akura did not take this path," remarked Tamara.

"I think you had much to do with that, my Dear," approved Sean.

Smiling, Tamara put her head on his shoulder. "So where do we go with this intel now?" she asked.

"I will teleport to Divos and meet with the mediators. Their input will put us on the right track," Sean predicted.

* * * * *

The next day, Sean returned to Akura and brought the mediators' recommendations to Tamara. "They are suggesting that, if we approve, their recommendations be formally presented to all parties in this dispute: both large, established kingdoms— and all the small communities scattered around Divos.

"One important recommendation is the establishment of an oversight agency composed of representatives from all affected parties. This agency would have the responsibility of assuring that the other recommendations are complied with in a fair and just manner," he concluded.

Tamara studied the document and found no fault in it. "This is excellent," she approved. "If the mediators can get all the parties to sign on, there is real hope for a good outcome."

"And if they can't?" worried Sean.

"Let's just trust the mediators to do their job," suggested Tamara. "They have a lot of experience to draw upon. I prefer to remain optimistic."

"I appreciate your positive attitude, my Dear," said Sean, smiling. "I'll teleport back to Divos in the morning…and then we wait."

Chapter 9
The Mediators Speak

Back on Divos, Sean had a private meeting with the mediators, who were pleased that Queen Tamara endorsed the entire list of their recommendations. The next step forward would be to present the list to all of the involved parties.

A schedule was prepared that would enable the entire group of mediators to meet with each affected kingdom and community. As the mediators embarked on their mission, their spirits were high. Hope was in the air.

Since the opinions of the representatives from the two kingdoms were well-known, the mediators decided to begin their mission by visiting the planet's small communities. Their views and needs had never been considered in the past.

Seeking out the wide range of concerns of these diverse populations proved to be very challenging...but also very informative. It took longer than they had anticipated, but the intel was golden.

Now perhaps their greatest set of potential obstacles lay before them: the two kingdoms that had dominated the planet unobstructed in recent memory. The mediators decided to face them head on…they prepared a summary of what they had learned from the numerous small communities. This intel would contain ideas and complaints that had never been presented to the kingdoms before. Could hardened attitudes be changed?

Days passed without any reports from the mediators. Sean was beginning to worry that the mission was in danger of imploding. Then, on a bright sunny day, the mediators surfaced and requested to be teleported to Explorer 1.

Sean was informed immediately and he teleported from his office in Marinea to join them. Explorer 1 contained a large room capable of accommodating everyone. As Sean entered, he looked intently at the faces of the mediators to try and gauge their mood.

He waved his hand and the room was filled with enough chairs for everyone, surrounding a large table. Waiting patiently for all the mediators to be comfortably seated, Sean allowed multiple scenarios to pass through his mind. Finally, he asked, "Have you any questions for me?"

The Lead Mediator shook his head and handed Sean a report, which he scanned quickly. "You have signatures from every affected group. How did you manage that?" Sean inquired with awe in his voice.

As one, the mediators smiled. A female mediator explained,

"Once we realized that the key to everyone's understanding was rooted in the land and its resources, we were able to move on and explore everyone's needs and desires. From there, our experience as mediators took over and negotiations became possible."

The Lead Mediator added, "It also helped that the Ruler of Dubbell was under house arrest. Without his interference, feelings of discomfort with his leadership began to arise and we were able to smooth the way to more equitable paths forward.

"In the documents I gave you, you will find additional recommendations for shared governance around the planet, including many possible models that are successful in other situations in the universe. When the various groups realized that we were offering informed recommendations and were not imposing rules or mandates, everyone seemed to relax and we made excellent progress.

"We will leave three mediators on Divos to be resources for the decisions that will need to be made: one in each of the two major kingdoms and a third available to the smaller communities," he concluded.

Sean stood and walked around the table, shaking every mediator's hand. He praised their skill and patience in confronting a difficult mission. He summoned Captain Kert to join them and requested cabins for the mediators who would be returning to Akura. He planned to personally teleport the three who will remain on Divos to their new assignments. Meanwhile, waving his hand, he produced a celebratory array of food and drink. It had been a very satisfying day.

*   *   *   *   *

That evening, Sean invited Tamara to join him in the Palace Garden for another walk. He had settled the three reassigned mediators in their new quarters on Divos and then teleported home with the ex-Ruler of Dubbell in his custody. That Ruler was now incarcerated temporarily with the spies that had been rounded up on Akura. Permanent disposition of the detainees was yet to be decided.

As Sean and Tamara strolled through the garden, they spoke at length about the successful use of mediation on Divos. Tamara praised the performance of the mediators and suggested that their use might be a frequent strategy in this intergalactic universe that they were now a part of.

"By the way, Dear," added Tamara, "The new General Manager of the Council of Kingdoms has been chosen. It will be Queen Astrid of Seaside. She was a clear choice."

Finding a vacant bench, they produced a bottle of bubbly and settled in for a victory lap!

Chapter 10

Family Matters

Tamara had reserved the Private Dining Room for the next night's dinner. She wanted to have her family around her…it seemed so long since that was possible. Affairs of State kept getting in the way!

She intended to gather everyone together, starting from when she was a child living in the kingdom of Alteria—before the Great Quakes that created the undersea kingdom of Marinea. Therefore, the first names on her invitation list were her mother, Terra, her father, Trident, and her younger sister, Trina.

Once she was swept away in the Quakes, two more names needed to be added: Solange and Savea, the Super Sisters who were her mentors as she adapted to her new surroundings.

Her family had grown so much since she was crowned Queen. She had met and wed Sean, the Commander of the Security Force. When she had first become pregnant, she expected to have one small babe to raise. Instead, she and Sean were blessed with

FOUR—and they were all Super Children with powers.

Now those first-born children were all wed and some had babes of their own:

1. Candace, the Queen-Designate, had wed Cyril, Ruler of Freedom and they were parents of Joy. Joy had accelerated her growth, wed Nolan, and produced Savvy and Starr—both of whom had also decided to boost their growth.

2. Sunny had wed Cyril's Super Brother, Cyrus, also from Freedom. They had not as yet produced children.

3. Skye had wed Greta from Marinea. They also did not have children.

4. Verd had wed Savea, one of the two original Super Sisters from Marinea. Years later, when a host of Super Twins were born to members of the family, Verd and Savea had Super twin sons, Lavan and Wavan.

At that time, Tamara and Sean also welcomed Super twin girls, Leilani and Andrea.

Her sister, Trina, had wed Jon from Marinea. They had twin Super sons, Tristan and Brendan.

Her Grandmother, Solange, had wed Sostor, Ruler of Mosshire. They had twin Super daughters, Coral and Frosti.

As always, her head was beginning to hurt while she tried to correctly remember multiple facts and relationships. One thing was certain: she was the Matriarch of a very extensive family! Her Journey down Memory Lane had also reminded her of the extensive influence of crystals on her family.

The invitations were issued and Tamara took a deep breath, confirming the detailed menu plans for the gathering. She was hopeful that everyone would be able to attend this special and long-awaited event.

*   *   *   *   *

It was the day of the family gathering. Tamara had awakened that morning and, when she looked in her bedroom mirror, the Pendant of Power she received when she was identified as a Super Child, looked different. She knew that Pendants of Power could not be removed, so she didn't usually pay much attention to hers. However, her Pendant now was encircled by a ring of rainbow colored crystals!

She called out for Mia, her personal attendant. Mia knocked softly at the door and rushed to her side. "Good morning, Your Majesty, How can I help you?"

"Look at my Pendant of Power," implored Tamara. "It has changed significantly. Do you have any idea why?"

Mia touched the Pendant and jumped back. "It just shocked me! That's new!"

Tamara sent a mental summons to Sean, urging him to come

to her. In a moment, he had teleported in. "What is wrong, Dear?" he asked.

"Has your Pendant of Power changed?" she inquired, her voice trembling.

Sean opened his shirt, exposing his Pendant. It looked the same as it always had. Tamara reached her hand out and touched it—and it morphed into one that looked like hers!

"Mother!!!" Tamara cried.

*   *   *   *   *

Terra, Tamara's mother and also Head Watcher, heard her daughter call out in panic. She hurried to confer with the Creator Being, who allayed her fears. Learning that this was actually a gift to celebrate the family at their gathering, Terra relaxed and teleported to her daughter's side.

Terra hugged Tamara, casting a calming spell. "Nothing is amiss, Dear," she soothed. "The Creator Being is bestowing a gift in celebration of our family."

Sean led Tamara to a nearby couch and created chairs for Terra and Mia. Tamara's voice quivered as she asked her mother, "Do you know what the multi-colored ring of crystals is supposed to do?"

"I didn't ask because I hadn't seen them," replied Terra, "but I will be sure to find out."

"When Sean arrived, his Pendant looked normal—until I touched it," added Tamara. "Are you wearing your Pendant, Mother?"

"Of course," Terra said, "It's not removable." She opened her shirt to expose the Pendant, which had not changed. Tamara reached over and touched it—a flash of light and her mother's Pendant had a rainbow ring!

"It seems, Dear," commented Terra, "that it's your touch which activates the change. I'll check with the Creator Being…but meanwhile, you may want to add some acknowledgement or ceremony to tonight's festivities!" And she vanished.

Chapter 11
The Family Celebration

Tamara was dressing for the family dinner when her mother returned. "I was right," confirmed Terra, "that you, as official family Matriarch, are the trigger for upgrading a Pendant. The Creator Being assured me that the rainbow ring signifies an increase in personal power, each color related to an ability. It will be up to us to experiment with the colors to discover just how and when new abilities surface."

Tamara invited her mother to sit by her on the couch. She wanted to share an idea for this evening that would introduce the Pendant change to everyone. As she described the ceremony she had planned, to take place in the Throne Room, Terra smiled in approval.

"That's quite a dramatic introduction, Tamara," Terra smiled. "When all the Pendants have changed, do you want me to share what the Creator Being told me?"

"I was hoping you would offer, Mother," Tamara responded with a hug.

*   *   *   *   *

It was almost time for the gathering to begin. Tamara had

requested that a series of signs giving directions be placed in the hall leading to the Throne Room. She knew her family would be puzzled by this maneuver, but they would eventually understand.

Tamara took her place on the throne at the end of the room. Soft music was playing and servers were busy distributing glasses of bubbly as family members arrived.

Another series of signs directed guests to walk toward the throne where Tamara was seated. As each person approached, Tamara stood and touched their Pendant of Power. A flash of light confirmed that the change had taken place.

When all family members had been 'upgraded', she led them into the Private Dining Room for dinner. As they settled into chairs around multiple tables, Tamara smiled and handed a communications device to her mother. The music temporarily paused as Terra began to tell a story…a story of their family and the many blessings and adventures that they had experienced.

She explained that their Pendants of Power had been upgraded by the Creator Being as a tribute to their family. Emphasizing that the altered Pendants would increase each person's personal power, Terra added that the nature of that power would be one of discovery and sharing among family members. The Rainbow Ring of crystals, as she called it, might operate using individual colors, or possibly in combination. That was yet to be determined.

"This was an unexpected gift from the Creator Being," she added, "and Tamara discovered it quite by accident when she awakened this morning."

Taking her seat next to Tamara, Terra smiled as a buzz of excited conversation swept through the Dining Room. "Mother, I have a feeling that this 'upgrade' is the beginning of a significant change," Tamara began. "Can you find out if I'm imagining it…or if something is really coming?"

"I will try, Dear," replied Terra, "but you know how the Creator Being operates…with subtlety."

"I hardly think that this 'upgrade' to our Pendants of Power is a subtle move," objected Tamara. "I feel uneasy about the future."

Sean, who was seated on Tamara's other side, took her hand and reminded her that whatever would lie ahead, they would face it together.

*   *   *   *   *

The evening proceeded smoothly through the dinner phase and entered a more informal afterglow. Luscious desserts appeared that could be transferred to the multiple new tables that appeared. Servers kept the bubbly flowing and family members moved around the room, interacting with others. Sean noticed that the purple crystal on his Pendant glowed as he conversed with other family members. He brought this to everyone's attention; the first discovery of power had been identified!

As the evening progressed, other crystals began to glow and their owners shared their discoveries. Tamara noticed that her family members were enjoying the interactions; it had almost become a game! She drifted from small group to small group, having the opportunity to share the celebration with everyone.

Beginning to relax, the worries slipped off Tamara's shoulders and she joined Sean in his stroll around the room. She thought to herself that there really should be more opportunities to enjoy the company of her family members. As that revelation surfaced, she felt a sudden disturbance in the air and…

She and Sean were in the Crystal Castle. Looking around, they saw Adele and Jeremy—the current Super Beings—at the top of the crystal staircase, waving that they should climb up and join them. With puzzled looks on their faces, Tamara and Sean ascended the staircase.

Chapter 12
Change is Coming

"Don't worry about the family," advised Jeremy. "They won't notice your absence. Remember that Time moves differently up here."

"We felt your awareness, Tamara, of wishing to spend more time with your family members," added Adele. "We've been waiting for the desire to surface."

"And I need to remind you that you also have family here in the Castle," Jeremy prodded. "Rogere, one of our two Watcher/Guardians, is your Grandfather, Tamara."

"Oh!" cried Tamara, "I should have invited him to the gathering!"

"He understands, Dear," Adele admonished. "Here he comes now, with Elsa, his wife and the other Watcher/Guardian."

"Oh no!" Tamara moaned, "I missed her, too. I'm so sorry."

"Everything is as it should be, Tamara," said Elsa. "You have served as Matriarch for a long time and your accomplishments are many. The Creator Being has decided that your duties on the arc of Time have been completed…and Adele's and Jeremy's as Super Beings have, as well. Your paths are about to change."

"I knew it!" exclaimed Tamara. "I could feel change coming! What if I/we are not ready?" She looked at Sean with tears in her eyes.

"You're not dying, Granddaughter," laughed Rogere. "You are being promoted!"

"Adele and Jeremy have been promoted to Emeritus status and will be housed in another part of the Castle. You and Sean will be the new Super Beings," explained Elsa. "The four of you will be working together to create a new order."

"That number FOUR again!" Tamara sighed. "What do you mean by 'a new order'?"

"You will return to your party and begin to institute the necessary changes," Rogere began. "The first, and most obvious one, will be the coronation of Candace as Queen. Then another Queen-Designate must be appointed."

Tamara blanched. This was becoming too real. "What about our Security Force? Sean is the Commander."

"Don't worry, Tamara," answered Sean. "We have an order of succession in place. Jon will resign the Academy Presidency and take over. This will be like Dominos…As each vacancy occurs and a new person takes office, another vacancy will happen. It will be a lengthy process overall."

Rogere spoke next. "When my son abdicated the throne of Marinea, you took over, Tamara—and did an outstanding job. Have faith in your daughter. She is ready."

Tamara began to sway, "I think I have to sit down." Sean assisted her to a nearby chair and stayed by her side.

"Everyone in this room will be involved in the changeover," promised Elsa. "After it is accomplished, the Emeritus Super Beings will be available to you as needed. Now it is time for you to return to your family gathering.

"You may inform the family of what is coming, but we recommend that you tell Candace first. She is the lynch pin of the process."

Sean helped Tamara to stand…and, suddenly, they were back in the Private Dining Room. He tucked her arm into his and resumed their stroll around the room. Leaning into her, he whispered that they would talk to Candace tomorrow.

*   *   *   *   *

The next day, Sean went to Tamara's office and they attempted to recreate what they had learned in the Crystal Castle the day before. After a while, they both had to admit that it had come as a shock; they had never been even close to retiring. Tamara had to admit, however, that she had experienced a desire to be closer to members of her family. That may have been just what the Creator Being had needed to prompt this looming change.

In tears, Tamara felt like it was all her fault. Sean tried to disabuse her of that idea, but it wasn't working. As a last resort, he sent an urgent summons to Terra, who appeared right away.

After further discussion, Terra winked out of sight, returning in a short time after visiting the Creator Being. She reported that no one had prompted yesterday's events in the Crystal Castle. Apparently, those plans had been in the works for some time. In the Creator Being's mind, it was a fortuitous moment to begin the change sequence. While there might be some distress temporarily, the ultimate outcome would be desirable for all concerned.

Tamara couldn't believe what she was hearing. Not only was she unhappy about the proposed change sequence, but now she realized that she was charged to direct its implementation. Sean put his arms around her and let her cry for awhile.

Terra contributed by casting a calming acceptance spell, hoping that would help. She also offered to assist with the inevitable transitions. When Tamara's tears lessened, her mother held her for awhile. They would need to rely on each other's strength to survive the days ahead. None of them noticed that the blue crystals on their Pendants were pulsing.

Chapter 13
First Steps

Tamara intended to talk to Candace today—as soon as she could gain control of her emotions. Terra released Tamara from the hug and led her to a nearby couch. As she helped Tamara settle into a comfortable position, Terra observed that the blue crystal on her own Pendant was throbbing...then she felt light-headed. Tamara cried out as her mother vanished.

Tamara had often watched her mother disappear—but not exactly like this. It was as if her mother had been summoned. Sean had seen the whole thing and he rushed to Tamara's side. Holding her, he cast a calming spell and chanted softly.

*   *   *   *   *

Meanwhile, Terra found herself in the company of the Creator Being. It was not unusual for her to visit, but this was the first visit that she did not initiate.

In her mind, she received a message from the Creator Being, apologizing for how the Crystal Castle episode the day before had been handled. Terra agreed that it could have been done better—and let that opinion be known.

She felt a second message being formulated and let it flow through her. It was long and complex, containing images of the two former Super Beings and the self-absorbed way they had lived in the Castle.

In a third message, she became acutely aware of the need to have Super Beings in the Castle who were more concerned about the beings they supervised and the changing nature of the universe. This was the underlying basis for reaching out to Tamara and Sean.

The fourth and final message (ah, that number FOUR again!) charged her with helping her daughter and son-in-law understand the importance of their mission.

When she was released to return to be with Tamara, she was exhausted from the intensity of her visit with the Creator Being, but also inspired to transmit the importance of the Creator Being's concerns.

*   *   *   *

Terra materialized in Tamara's office and hurried to go to her. She was glad Sean was already sitting next to Tamara; she wanted both of them to hear what she had to say.

She opened her mind to them and let the intel flow. Watching their faces as they absorbed what the Creator Being had shared, Terra knew when the message had reached its goal.

The fear and distress that had plagued them was no longer present. Instead, a determination to follow the assigned mission glowed in their eyes. They understood why they were chosen and what they had to do.

First on their list was to speak with Candace, the Queen-Designate. Tamara sent her a mental summons and then she and Sean sat back to wait.

Candace was always prompt. It was only a few minutes before she was knocking on the door. "Is everything all right, Mama?" she asked.

Tamara opened her mind and the intel flowed into Candace, who blanched as she began to swoon. Sean extended his arms and steered Candace toward the couch. When she had recovered her senses, she stared at her parents in disbelief.

"I thought I had a long time before this day," Candace sighed. "But I understand the Creator Being's urgency. However, beyond that, I want to point out to both of you that you are also being rewarded for long years of exemplary service. And you deserve it!"

She smiled at her parents as she stiffened her spine and prepared to change her life. Tamara and Sean gazed at their daughter with pride. She would, indeed, make a fantastic Queen…and she was ready!

*   *   *   *   *

At dinner that evening, Candace and Cecil had joined her parents for advance planning. She had also invited Sunny and Cyrus to join them, since Sunny was presently the second-in-line for the throne. Some immediate decisions needed to be made.

Once Tamara had fully-informed Sunny of the upcoming changes, Sunny looked very thoughtful and then proclaimed, "When we were establishing the rules of succession, my position was contingent upon yours, Candy. Succession ran from Grandpa to Mama to you...all in the same familial line. When you are crowned Queen, the line will continue on through YOUR offspring. I will no longer be a direct descendent."

Candace looked stunned, then the stark realization hit her—Sunny was right! But she needed verification and summoned her grandmother. Terra appeared in a flash of light. Once the proposed change in the order of succession was presented to her, she agreed that Sunny was correct.

"The revised order should pass through your oldest child: Joy," Terra confirmed. "She will be the Queen-Designate. I will send for her."

In a few moments, Joy and Nolan had joined the dinner party and the imminent changes were presented to them. "I knew this would happen, Mama," she acknowledged. "I have seen it. But it's sooner than I expected. I intend to remain a Space Force Captain, so we will have to work around that reality."

Tamara was rubbing her temples. Her famous headache had returned. She felt the world spinning around her...when she looked up, she and Sean were back in the Crystal Castle.

About the Author

After doing academic writing during my 20 years as Professor at the University of Wisconsin-Madison, I retired to Hawai'i in 1999. A decade later, I began being aware of an interesting fantasy story line in my mind and began writing it soon after. It was an occasional hobby for another decade and then the book became impatient with me and began to seriously nudge me. Since I began "listening" to the book, the writing has been a fun and all-encompassing part of my life.

I have completed 12 books in my Crystal Saga Series 1 and 12 books in Crystal Saga Series 2. I have completed books 1 through 12 in my Crystal Saga Series 3 and I have now complete Books 1 and 2 in Series 4 with books 3 and 4 right on their heels. As always, stay tuned for more adventures.

Crystal Saga Series 1 by
D. E. Weingand

Book 1 — Tamara's Crystals

Book 2 — Genesis Explored

Book 3 — Masquerade

Book 4 — Discoveries

Book 5 — Gamesmanship

Book 6 — Beginnings

Book 7 — Looking Forward . . . and Backward

Book 8 — Making Progress

Book 9 — Searching for Truth

Book 10 — The Truth is Out There

Book 11 — Finding Truth

Book 12 — Loose Ends

Scan the QR Code with Your Cell Phone to Order Books. Or go to LuLu.com, Amazon.com, Barnsandnoble.com and many other outlets.

Crystal Saga Series 2 by
D. E. Weingand

Book 1 — Exploration

Book 2 — More Mysteries

Book 3 — Escalation

Book 4 — Renewals

Book 5 — New Beginnings

Book 6 — More Crystals

Book 7 — The World Changes

Book 8 — Romance Blossoms

Book 9 — New (Ad)Ventures

Book 10 — (Ad)Ventures Continue

Book 11 — Designing the Future

Book 12 — The Future Beckons

Crystal Saga Series 3 by
D. E. Weingand

Book 1 — The Next Generations

Book 2 — Into the Future

Book 3 — The Fourth Generation

Book 4 — Starlight

Book 5 — Exploring Starlight

Book 6 — The Planet of Starlight

Book 7 — The Saga of Planet X . . . and Beyond

Book 8 — What's Next?

Book 9 — Dealing with Darkness

Book 10 — Expansion into Space

Book 11 — Explorer 1

Book 12 — Explorer 2

Crystal Saga Series 4 by
D. E. Weingand

Book 1 — Defense = Offense

Book 2 — Interplanetary Conflict

Coming Soon

Book 3 — The New Order

Book 4 — Adapting to Change